for Ashtin —

A Taste

OF HONEY

sweets to the sweet! ♥

ROSE LERNER

A TASTE OF HONEY
Copyright ©2017 by Susan Roth

Cover by Kanaxa

roselerner.com

Table of Contents

For everyone
who read Sweet Disorder
AND TOLD ME THEY WOULD HAVE
MARRIED MR. MOON.

Acknowledgments

First, I would like to thank my wonderful friends and first readers: Tiffany Ruzicki, Olivia Waite, and Susanna Fraser. You are everything.

I want to thank all the people out there researching and recreating historical food, with a special shout-out to Ivan Day of historicfood.com for his incredible work in Georgian sugar sculptures and ice cream.

Thank you to Alyssa Everett for founding the Demimonde critique group and for floating the idea, a long time ago, that we do an erotic novella anthology. I would never have thought of this story without that push.

Thank you to Kanaxa for another improbably gorgeous cover, and Matt Youngmark for another elegant formatting job. I am so lucky to have you.

As always, thank you to my family for their support and for always taking romance seriously.

Thank you to my readers. I love visiting Lively St. Lemeston with you.

And of course, thank you to Sonia, my other half.

CHAPTER 1:

Tuesday

LIVELY ST. LEMESTON, WEST SUSSEX
JULY 1813

R obert Moon stood at the low fire stirring a copper kettle of boiling sugar, coffee, and cream. It was nearly to caramel height, and a good thing too, for Robert had been standing there far too long. His skin itched with a combination of dripping sweat and all the things he'd ought to do instead.

This task belonged to his apprentice Peter Makepeace, but Peter's great-aunt was ill in London and like to die, and the Makepeaces had begged to take him up North in hopes she'd remember the lad in her will.

Maybe I hadn't ought to have agreed, Robert thought for the thousandth time in two days.

He'd got spoiled, having someone about to do all the things he'd rather not. Of course he couldn't deny Peter this chance.

Dipping his finger into the bowl of cold water behind him, he dipped it quickly in the pot, and back in the water. The sugar slipped off and floated, hardening. But it stuck to his teeth. He wiped the sweat from his face and stirred on.

The doorbell rang at the front of the shop. Betsy's voice

welcomed a customer, a cheerful murmur he couldn't make out.

He knew how she'd look, the hopeful arch of her eyebrows and sunny bow of her lips, the soft curve of her cheek as she tilted her head. The sweet flare of her hips under her gown and apron. He wished he could see it.

He wished Peter were here. Alone in the great oven of a kitchen, hours behind where he'd ought to be, how could he even daydream that the shop would ever succeed far enough that he could ask Betsy to marry him? The Honey Moon brought in more money than half a year ago—but half a year ago he'd been *this* close to…

He tried not to think the word, made an empty space in his mind where it had been. The emptiness was still the shape of the word, though.

Bankruptcy.

He turned back to his sugar. Even-almost ready…

Betsy pushed through the swinging door. The summer sun turned her hair yellow as an apple, and her hazel eyes were bright and warm with excitement.

"It's Mrs. Lovejoy. She might want *us* to make the collation for next week's assembly! I told her she'd ought to speak with you, Mr. Moon. She wants it settled on the spot." Out of the corner of his eye, he saw Betsy's longsuffering shrug.

Mrs. Lovejoy, wife of a wealthy wholesaler who sat on the Lively St. Lemeston Assembly Rooms' governing committee, was one of their bettermost customers, if bettermost was measured in guineas. Robert wondered now and again if her money really paid for the many hours he and Betsy had spent with her, coddling and courting and nodding sympathetically at complaints.

The bakery in Runford had had its share of difficult customers, but Robert was still sometimes shocked at how the rich folk here, used to getting what they wanted, could carry on.

Well, that was his own fault for opening a shop that sold expensive things. As Betsy always said, *If people can murder each other, it hadn't ought to shock you when they're a bit rude now and again.* Robert knew a loyal customer like Mrs. Lovejoy gave returns that couldn't be measured only in what she herself bought.

And here was the proof of it: the collation for an assembly would bring in a whacking sum, and put his sweets in the mouths of dunnamany of the town's wealthiest folks.

Could he manage the work without Peter?

He tested the caramel once more. Still a touch shy of crackly.

"I'm in a hurry, Mr. Moon," Mrs. Lovejoy called from the front.

He could see no help for it. "It's eenamost ready. You've to tend it."

Betsy drew back. "But I've never—"

"Faith, it's simple. You've only to dip your finger in water, and the sugar, and the water again, and when it shatters like glass between your teeth, it's done. Take it off the fire and pour it in that tin plate, and roll it flat with the buttered rolling pin."

"But—"

"Let her once in the kitchen, and we'll never be rid of her."

Betsy couldn't argue with that. She took the spoon with an adorable quiver of her mouth.

Robert wanted to give her a reassuring touch. He gave her a smile instead. "I'll be back in no more'n a hundred years or so, never fear."

Mrs. Lovejoy stood at the counter, in nervesome fidgets. Her face brightened when she saw him. "Oh, Mr. Moon! You'll never believe what my husband has done. He was charged with ordering the collation for next week's assembly, and the fool clean forgot. How he could when the whole town is talking of nothing *but* the assembly, I'm sure I don't know. But that's men for you."

Robert smiled politely. "We struggle against our natures, Mrs. Lovejoy."

She smiled back. Was that a slight flutter of her eyelashes? He hoped not. "The smell in here is calming my nerves as it always does. I always say, the Honey Moon is a refuge. Sometimes I can't hear myself think in the flipper-de-flapper out there, and then I come into your shop and smell delicious things and I can breathe again."

"Thank you, ma'am. That's exactly what I wanted when I opened the place. Now tell me about the assembly. How many folk are you expecting?"

She sighed heavily. "You never know with these country assemblies, do you? I told my husband we ought to keep it the second of August. We've had it then ever since the Battle of the Nile in 1798, and we've had good luck with that date. But nothing would suit the *newer* members of the committee but that we have it straightaway in June to celebrate Wellington and Vitoria."

She leaned in confidingly. "Well, the poor creatures have no experience organizing such large affairs, do they? It's all political to them. They prefer Wellington above Nelson because his brother is quarreling with the Prime Minister over the Catholic question."

Since the Battle of Vitoria was cause for jubilation across

all of Europe that wasn't yet under the Corsican Monster's thumb, Robert wondered if that might be a trifle unfair. But faith, you could never tell. Politics in Lively St. Lemeston was like watching French chefs argue over the bettermost way to make gravy.

"In the end the best we could do was compromise, and so we're having it next Tuesday. The date has no significance to anyone at all, so who can say who will bother to turn up? And then Mr. Lovejoy forgot about the supper entirely. It will be a disastrous evening if we can't save it." She leaned in further, as if they were coconspirators.

After several more minutes of wheedling, she owned that she was expecting between one and two hundred guests. Robert would have to make enough for two hundred twenty-five at least; running out was unthinkable. Could it be done in a week?

"There'll have to be ices," she said. "Ices, or I go elsewhere. Ices will make everyone forget what a dreadful hot evening they're having." She smiled archly.

Robert smiled back uneasily. Ices were a punishment to transport, and they couldn't be hardened in large molds if they weren't to be served and divided at once. Everyone would want some, which meant two hundred twenty-five individual ices in ice chests, and in this heat it might be an hour and a half to properly congeal one batch.

Still, the Assembly Rooms were just down the street, to the other side of Market Square and a bit.

"How much were you hoping to spend?" he asked.

"Oh, not above twenty-five pounds."

Robert swallowed, struck dumb.

Twenty-five pounds—and out-and-out, guaranteed! Not

having to be hoped and haggled and nipped for. Twenty-five pounds would keep the bailiffs from the door a few more months at least.

He'd risked his all to open this shop: sold his great-grandfather's bakery, leased premises on the main street of the biggest town in the district. Most eateries that opened failed, and the few that did make money generally only did so after they'd been open for years. But Robert had got this far, and he'd done it by snatching every chance he could and making the best sweets he knew how.

He'd never tasted ices to beat his own. If he could do this...

Betsy poked her head through the swinging door, looking frowzy and red and miserable. Damp strands of blond hair clung to her forehead.

"Mr. Moon," she said, so quiet he almost couldn't hear her.

He knew what she was going to tell him already. "Can you pour it off and save what's on top?"

She hung her head. "I scraped it off the bottom without realizing. It's through and through. I'm that sorry."

He did his best to smile at her. "Set her on the table then. I'll be in soon as ever I can. We'll make burnt caramel sauce instead."

That was at least a shillingsworth more cream and coffee, to thin it down, and the sauce sure to go grainy before they could sell enough cake to top with it.

"I like that girl," Mrs. Lovejoy said softly when the door had stopped swinging, "but she isn't very bright, is she? You ought to find somebody better. You owe it to yourself."

"Betsy does very well," he said, sharper than he meant to. "I've burnt dunnamuch caramel in my time. It's only a second or two this way and that."

It made him sick to his stomach every time, all that sweet, rich labor and love gone to ruin in the blink of an eye. Oh, folks liked burnt caramel all right. But it always killed him to know what could have been, if he'd only done it right.

He'd ought to say no to Mrs. Lovejoy. He'd ought to just struggle on slowly and quietly, like the tortoise in the fable. It was folly to take this order. He'd have to close the shop all week and work on nothing else, with no help but Betsy's. She was a clever girl whatever Mrs. Lovejoy thought, but she wasn't a confectioner.

But Robert didn't want to go slowly and quietly. If he could do this, maybe by the end of the year, or by next summer, he could ask Betsy to marry him.

"I'd be that honored, ma'am, thank you," he said. "You won't regret it."

"And he wants me to help him!" Betsy finished in triumph. "This is my chance."

Her friend Jemima looked unimpressed. "Your chance to do what, pray? Besides slave at a hot fire all the livelong day." She set aside the *Lively St. Lemeston Intelligencer* with a sigh and picked up the *Times*. "No murders in Sussex this week."

Every Tuesday, when the town newspaper came out, they met at the Makepeaces' coffeehouse to go through all the week's papers for interesting crimes.

Today they'd been obliged to go to the Cocoa Seedling since all the Makepeaces were in London. Jemima was just out of sorts at having to give Tories her hard-earned coin for such weak coffee.

"Here's a haunting that could have been a murder." Betsy passed the *Evening Chronicle* across the table. "If two people fall mysteriously down the stairs at one inn, and each time the sole witness is the innkeeper's wife, maybe the coroner hadn't ought to be so certain-sure it's a ghost. Anyways, you know what I mean. My chance to prove that a wife's not a burden and an expense. A wife is a helpmeet."

She felt hot, and ashamed all over again, thinking on the morning's caramel ignominy. "I'll do everything perfect, and he'll realize he needs me."

Jemima rolled her eyes. "You've been mooning after him for how long? He took the first moment when he hired you to let drop—oh, no reason why, just for something to say—that he weren't looking for a wife, and then he eenamost married that widow for money. What makes you think he'd like to marry you at all?"

Betsy pressed her lips together. Jemima had been patient and encouraging about this at first. But that was more than a year ago now. And Jemima had taken it hard, harder even than Betsy, when Robert had courted another woman.

He hadn't loved Mrs. Sparks—Mrs. Dymond now, of course. He'd only done it because the Whig patroness of the town had promised to pay his debts, for marriage to Mrs. Dymond would have made him a voter under the town charter and votes were a precious commodity.

But it had still hurt, and Jemima couldn't forgive that.

"He told me that because he shouldn't like to raise false hopes. Because he likes me. I can tell." Betsy hoped. "He's that sweet, he wouldn't want to see someone he loved do without. What he said was, he wouldn't take a wife *until the Honey Moon is a success*. The sooner we can make a success of it, the sooner—"

Jemima's straight dark brows drew together harshly. "Or he's a coward who weaseled out of having to say he didn't want you."

Betsy's heart sank. What if Jemima had the right of it?

"You already good as run that shop," her friend said. "You don't need him to see you as a helpmeet. You need him to see you as a *woman*."

Betsy's heart popped up again and peered hopefully about. "Do you think so?"

Jemima nodded like her head was on a hinge. She knew whereof she spoke; Betsy always wondered a little that boys, who seemed a timid lot on the whole, weren't frightened off by her square jaw and piercing dark gaze, but she had a new beau every week.

"I couldn't—I couldn't *seduce* him." Betsy flushed. "I'd feel that silly."

Jemima waved this away. "Seducing a man just means letting him know you'd kiss him back if he tried it. And then kissing him yourself, if he's too shy. You needn't bunger about licking your lips or leaning over to show him your tits. Just smile at him, look him in the eye, and make a few dirty jokes so he knows you know what's what. It's not as if Robert Moon's had all sorts of beautiful women chucking themselves at him. You'll do fine."

Betsy couldn't help a sorrowful inkling that that advice would do very well for Jemima, but wouldn't suit *her* at all. She saw her own apple-cheeked face in the mirror every morning—if a bit dimly, as it wasn't a very good mirror.

She was pretty enough, but if she were a flower, she'd be a daisy, if she were a bird, she'd be a robin, and if she were a pastry, she wouldn't be a French pastry, or even a rich dark honey bun. She was simple and wholesome as a fresh-baked roll. The only remotely wicked thing about her was that she enjoyed shivering over *The Newgate Calendar, or, the Malefactors' Bloody Register*.

But she'd kiss Robert Moon back if he tried it.

Heat flared inside her at the thought, low and hungry and not simple or wholesome at all. "All right, I will."

Jemima smiled. "Good on you."

She would. She'd whiled away enough time meekly waiting for him to notice her. She'd make him see her as a woman, she'd bed him if he was willing, and then, if he still hadn't asked her to marry him when the assembly was over, she'd give her two weeks' notice and find somewheres else to work.

And she'd have memories to take with her.

CHAPTER 2:

Wednesday

B etsy latched the kitchen door, checked it twice, then tied her apron on and went straight to work scalding and blanching almonds for macaroons. It was strange, coming to the Honey Moon and not opening up the shop.

It was strange as well, knowing she planned on seducing Mr. Moon. Strange to look at his familiar face and think, *I'm going to kiss him*, and not how lovely it would be if he asked her to go walking with him. It made her feel powerful, humming with could-bes and just-maybes. It also made the pit of her stomach wobble like jelly with nerves.

After two and a half hours' knabbling, Mr. Moon and Mrs. Lovejoy had shook hands on a menu of two great strawberry trifles, four big raspberry cream tarts, peaches in brandy, plums and cherries in molded jelly, sponge biscuits and macaroons, and ices for two hundred and fifty, with the *pièce montée* to be a Greek temple of paste and blancmange, its burnt-cream terrace surrounded by a pistachio-cream lawn and rock-candy boulders, the whole ornamented with candied flowers.

"I've to order all our fruit and cream and butter," he told her, and off he went, leaving her alone.

Betsy had been prepared to set her plan into motion straightaway. Her nerves jangled; she found herself thinking of all the ways someone could get in and abduct her from the closed shop. She set a paring knife and a heavy rolling pin on the counter beside her, and kept on slipping almonds from their skins.

Mr. Moon didn't reappear until eight, bringing bread and cheese to share and looking a little wide-eyed with anxiety. He hardly ate, and sifted her pounded sugar for lumps.

With an inward sigh, Betsy put off kissing him once again. "Mr. Moon," she said firmly, "you've got to break your fast."

"I had some coffee and a potato," he said absently. But under questioning, he confessed that had been at dawn, and he'd only eaten half the potato.

"You won't sleep much between now and Tuesday," Betsy pointed out. "You need your strength. A man can't live on coffee." She didn't point out how nervesome hunger made him.

He gave her a rueful glance and ate his bread and cheese.

Betsy felt warm. He needed her. If she were his wife, she could make him sleep too.

When he'd finished, he inspected her blanched almonds. Betsy held her breath until he smiled at her. "Fine work."

She knew she was glowing and tried not to think of what Jemima would say about that.

He bit his lip. "Do you know, the pastries will go stale afore we reopen."

Going to the front of the shop, he reappeared with the lemon custard pie, only missing three slices. He cut her a slavven, holding it out with a shy duck of his head.

Betsy melted a bit at the edges. The lemon custard was her favorite. And even though he knew it, even though he'd done her a kindness, he watched her face when she took a bite as if maybe this time, she wouldn't like it.

She hummed happily for his benefit. "Faith, it's better each time you make it. I know what I'll have for my elevener."

He broke into a smile and cut himself a piece, still watching her eat.

Betsy felt hot and crackly as a sugar topping under the salamander. Would he be so eager to please her when they coupled?

She met his eyes and licked sticky lemon custard from her lips. "Have I got it all?"

He flushed, eyes following her tongue. Was he interested, or only embarrassed? "I believe so."

"Would you mind looking closer? I hate to go about with something on my face."

He tilted up her chin into the light from the high windows and moved his head from side to side, his narrow gaze on her mouth. She let her lips part on a sigh.

"You've got a crumb," he said. His thumb came up, pulled back, hovered, then rubbed at a spot just below his own mouth. "Here."

"Thank you." She brushed it away, trying to meet his eyes and let him know she was in no hurry to end the moment. But he turned away hastily, ears bright red.

Somehow the back of his neck made her wild too.

The almonds had to be pounded fine in a mortar with orange-flower water. She and Mr. Moon set up side by a side at a table, the great heap of almonds between them.

Betsy had often thought there was something immodest in the motion of driving the pestle into the mortar—more so when she watched Mr. Moon's expert, forceful strokes, and his shoulder moving beneath his shirt. Even with most of the ovens banked, the linen clung damply to him.

Always before, she'd tried to put it from her mind. But Jemima had said, *Make a few dirty jokes, so he knows you know what's what.*

"This poor mortar," she said, glancing at him. "She'll be that sore in the morning."

Mr. Moon dropped his pestle with a clang. It rolled across the kitchen and under a table on the far side of the room.

By the time the macaroons were in the oven, Betsy had given up on subtlety. Mr. Moon was too honorable to take the hints she dropped in any practical way.

Jemima had said she might kiss him herself if he proved shy, but the difficulty was she was five foot one and he was near to six feet. She couldn't kiss him without his aid and abetment unless she first dragged over a crate and stood upon it.

What if she tried it, and he didn't bend down to meet her? She'd be trying to climb him like one of the overeager pugs customers sometimes brought into the store.

"We'd best get a start on the Naples biscuits," he said.

There was nothing for it. A week was pitifully scant time to win a man's heart. She couldn't allow this whole day to go by.

"In a moment," she said.

He frowned at her in puzzlement.

Betsy gulped. "It isn't often we're alone in the kitchen."

"It's odd not having Peter about, isn't it?" He chuckled. "And much more work for us."

Her muscles tightened with nerves—even her cunny, and

that made her ache delightfully all over. "I was hoping we might"—*meet his eyes, meet his eyes*—"take advantage of the opportunity." She couldn't quite smile.

Neither did he. It was rare that he stood so still. It made her feel as if she didn't know him at all.

"Take advantage of it how?" he asked slowly.

"I was hoping you might kiss me." The last few words were a squeak. Oh God.

There was a long silence. Betsy felt near tears. He didn't want to. He didn't want to and she'd have to leave. What would she tell her mother? Good jobs didn't grow upon trees.

He turned his face away. "You know I can't take a wife."

"You were ready enough to take a wife last autumn."

Oh, to take the words back! She'd meant to be a promise of enjoyment as sweet and undemanding as a slice of cake, and now she sounded like a nag.

He turned away further. "You know I only needed the money. I was this close to sending the bankruptcy notice to the *Intelligencer*, and marrying Mrs. Dymond would have stopped it. I can't—I might still have to send that notice, one of these days."

His eyes went round the shop, lingering on each bright copper mold as if losing even one would break his heart. She remembered how he'd hung them so carefully on their hooks when the shop was new, the look on his face when he'd stepped back. Proud and happy, as if he'd earned his heart's desire. He'd never look at her that way, would he?

He didn't say he didn't like you, she comforted herself. But Mr. Moon was the softest-hearted man she knew. He'd never admit he didn't like her if he had another reason he could give.

"I can go hungry, if I have to," he said. "I couldn't watch

my wife do it. And I've got debts of my own that bankruptcy wouldn't cancel out. I could bear to go to debtors' prison, if I wasn't leaving anybody behind that I was meant to keep and care for."

The injustice was hot coals in her stomach, that because she was poor and had no patronage to bring him, he wouldn't look at her. She'd never minded going without fine clothes or rich joints of meat, but she hated being unable to afford happiness.

He cracked an egg into a bowl with a vicious jerk of his wrist. "Nicholas Dymond can make a love match. A man like me…" His mouth drew tight. "And there I've got eggshell in the bowl." He reached in to pick it out, his lips whitening each time the shell eluded him.

More than she wanted to marry him, she wanted to ease his burden. She liked the shop well enough, but her reward for smiling at customers until her jaw ached, scrubbing gummy flour from the floor on hands and knees, forever tasting and smelling charcoal smoke—it was his smile, his relief at not having to do this alone.

He needed a bit of uncomplicated fun. Maybe it would even help him see that a wife was more than a weight on a man's shoulders.

"I didn't ask you to marry me. I asked you to kiss me."

He looked back at her. "But—I couldn't—you're a good girl, and—"

"I'm not a virgin," she blurted out.

It was only true in the barest sense. She'd let Lenny Sadler roger her a few times when they were both fourteen and his aunt was chambermaid in a house with a perpetual blood-stain, and he'd got her in to see it.

She'd wanted it at first, but she'd liked it much less than Lenny had, and he hadn't seemed overjoyed himself. Then she'd been terrified she was pregnant and cried herself to sleep every night until her monthly bleeding started.

She'd stayed clear of the whole business after that. Still, she wasn't a virgin.

Mr. Moon's eyes went round. Oh, what if he called her a slut and dismissed her without a character?

"You really only want me to kiss you?"

She licked her lips—not to be seductive but because they'd gone dry. "Well…not *only* kiss me."

He swallowed hard. There was another long silence. Surely he couldn't only be hunting for a kind way to turn her down?

She tried to look confident and tempting, to put nothing but *I want you to kiss me* on her face.

Robert looked down at Betsy, asking him to kiss her with her big hazel eyes.

She wasn't a virgin? She didn't want to marry him?

Panic filled him. He'd known he could lose her, that every moment he was obliged to delay was another chance for her to leave. But he'd never guessed that he'd maybe already lost her.

Had she been meeting other men all this time? He tried to decide if the idea disgusted him. It didn't.

Surely the idea of one's intended wife with another man ought to be repulsive, and not…exciting. Betsy, demure Betsy who worked cheerfully from dawn till dusk, had a secret life he knew naught about.

He hadn't known what to think when she'd said that about

the pestle. Now he wondered, did she speak from experience? Had there been mornings when she'd come in yawning to open the shop, sore and sated from being pounded by another man's cock?

He shouldn't think like this. He respected her. He *loved* her, and whatever she'd done with other men, he ought to treat her like a respectable woman.

But she said she wanted him to. She said they'd ought to take advantage of this opportunity, and she was right about one thing at least: who knew when they'd have another chance? Peter would be back soon.

If Robert gave her this, if he satisfied her, maybe she'd not mind waiting to marry. Maybe she wouldn't look elsewhere.

Maybe—he could barely let himself think it—maybe if he did well enough, she'd fall in love with him. Then she wouldn't wed someone else while he was waiting to see if the Honey Moon would ever turn a profit.

They'd be risking her reputation, but it seemed she was risking that already. And if she wasn't his wife, his creditors couldn't squeeze money from her. She could walk away if the shop closed.

She was so beautiful.

He could fill a ledger with reasons to kiss her, but it came down to this: he didn't have it in him to say no to her one more time. Not when she looked at him through her lashes like that, her breasts rising and falling as if she was trying to be calm and wasn't, not at all.

He grimaced.

Her face fell. "Never mind," she muttered. "I—"

"It's only that you'll have to show me what to do." His ears were hot. "You, erm—you might not be a virgin, but I be." He'd been busy. And shy.

"Oh."

Was it a disappointed 'oh'? "But I learn quick," he added hastily. "It can't be much trickier than a good pie crust."

She smiled as if that was funny.

He flushed harder. "I can make it good for you." It came out lower and more pleading than he'd meant it to. "I will. I promise."

Her lashes fluttered, and her mouth curved just a quarter-inch. Not amused this time. She looked as if she were about to bite into a chocolate caramel—the same rich, melting expectancy. "I know you will."

He leaned down—rather far down—and kissed her.

She tasted like lemon custard, and lurched about on her tiptoes. He tried to get closer, and she stepped back. When he did it again, thinking they'd fetch up against the wall, they almost tumbled through the swinging door into the cold room.

There was a bout of nervous giggling. Robert looked round and spied a solution to his trouble. "Come here."

Putting his hands round her arse, he lifted her onto the edge of an empty worktable. She flailed a little, but he stepped in before she could tip off.

Yes, now her mouth was only a few inches lower than his. Much better.

She pressed close, spreading her legs for balance, and he realized something else. Her cunt was just at the level of his cock. Could he—she'd said 'not *only* kiss'—could he really—?

One of her shoes clunked to the floor. Kicking off the other one, she tugged her skirts above her knees and wrapped her legs eagerly around him.

Ouch. His cock was trapped at an unpleasant angle in his

smallclothes.

"I, erm, I beg your pardon, but I—" He reached apologetically into his breeches to arrange his cock upright along his belly, where it cradled snugly in the juncture of her thighs. Dear Lord in Heaven.

"Oh," she said. "Pardoned. *Oh.*" She clasped her hands behind his neck and wriggled closer, tilting her hips up. "Oh, that's—I—" Her cheeks turned pink and she squeezed her eyes shut. "You don't mind?"

"Not in the slightest."

She edged forward, her lips parting in rapture. "Oh." Soft and eager, it was halfway between a word and a moan.

His own pleasure wasn't great—her movements were small and his breeches thick. But he could have watched her for hours, her creamy brow furrowed in concentration. The hollow between her breasts narrowed with each shallow gasp.

He took her arse in his hands again, squeezing, rubbing her against him. He'd never dreamed he'd be allowed to touch her like this. Not so soon, or so suddenly.

Her eyes flew open. "Oh—I'm going to—you're *sure* you don't mind?"

He made a choked sound. "I've—I've wanted you to. Dunnamany months now."

"You have?" Her mellow voice was thready with passion.

He nodded. "When you put something I cooked in your mouth, and you—you shut your eyes and sighed. I thought about what it would be like to give you—well, this."

He'd imagined all kinds of things. Her sharing his bed and board.

She couldn't stay the night, he realized, disappointed. He'd still be alone in his bed tonight, and every night for who knew how long.

She pinked, looking pleased. "Truly?"

He leaned down to kiss her. "Tru—" His eyes widened. "Wait! I've to look at the biscuits."

He'd almost forgot. He'd almost ruined them.

Three trays were round and golden; the fourth needed another half a minute. In agony he waited at the oven for them to darken, heart pounding, darting glances at her. Would she be patient? Was she annoyed at having her pleasure put off?

This was still Betsy, he reminded himself, not some courtesan with smooth white hands. She was a reasonable girl, and she understood about biscuits.

And to his relief, though she hunched nervesomely and rubbed at her arm, she stayed where she was, skirts above her knees. He caught her smiling once or twice, and she swung her legs like a carefree child.

At last the fourth tray was cooling on the counter. Had he ought to begin again where he left off, or had he better do something new?

"Will you…never mind." She bit her lip, looking at him and then away.

"I'm sure I will."

She shook her head.

"Tell me. I want to."

"I was going to ask if you would touch me. There. Only I'm afeared 'twill be—well. Messy."

He laughed. "Will it now?"

In truth, Robert had little notion what to expect. French engravings lacked detail, and he hadn't seen so very many of them as all that. Stepping back, he pushed her skirts out of the way with a touch of anxiety.

He saw fine golden hair and a strip of brownish pink flesh, wrinkled like a plump raisin. Hardly frightening. He ran his thumb through thick, slippery wetness.

She shivered, and he couldn't help smiling. "No worse'n egg whites. And I've never minded those."

Her laugh was a little self-conscious. "Oh, Robert Moon, you've got a silver tongue."

The word tongue put an idea in his head. "Would you—would you dislike me to kiss you there?"

She looked alarmed. Was that not a thing folk did? Robert couldn't be the only man to think of it.

"I don't know what it will taste like," she said.

"No way but one to find out."

"If it's awful…"

"I'll stop and eat a sweet." He reached up to a shelf for a jar of licorice drops, fishing one out and setting it on the counter in readiness. "There. I be prepared now."

She rolled her eyes and nodded, looking reassured.

Robert lowered himself to his knees on the floor, thinking this was an excellent reason to get flour on his breeches, not like dropping his pestle behind a table. He spread the folds of her cunt with his thumbs, to get a better look.

The smell was pleasant enough, musky and rich with a salty-smoky tang to it. Not like something you'd want to eat, but not like fish either, as people joked. He dipped his head to taste her.

She had a salty-smoky tang in his mouth too, and a hint of sourness. He skimmed the tip of his tongue along the edge of her slit.

She cried out in surprise and clutched at the table, hooking her legs over his shoulders for balance. When he licked the other side, her knuckles turned white.

"Are you sure it isn't awful?" she said in a faint voice.

"Quite sure." Robert felt smugly superior to the other men she'd bedded, who'd never thought of something so simple.

Exploring with his fingers, he discovered a small reddish-pink lump hidden by folds of skin, an inch above her slit. It looked almost angry. Curious, he licked it too.

Betsy gave a long, helpless moan, her hips tilting towards him like a flower to the sun.

Sucking the lump into his mouth, he licked again. Betsy panted, sinking back on her elbows. Her thighs shook on his shoulders.

So he kept going, feeling for her slick opening. His thumb slid in easily, not at quite the angle he'd ignorantly imagined.

"Ahh," Betsy moaned. "Ah-ah—"

She was tight even around his thumb. Could she really make space for his manhood? Her inner walls gave encouragingly when he pressed them. She was all aquiver now, her moans feverish, not at all like the mild, friendly girl he knew. He frigged her with his thumb in a mimicry of coupling, his mouth on that tiny lump.

"Please. Please..." He thought there must be something more she wanted, but a moment later she said, "Oh—yes—yes—I don't know if I'd ought—"

Her cunt tugged at his thumb hard, startling him. There was a pause, and then all at once she was boiling over, her heels drumming on his back, her insides rippling with astonishing strength.

So this was woman's pleasure. Robert could hardly breathe for thinking of his cock inside her. That strength was meant to carry his seed to her womb.

He felt a pang at the thought, and tried to quash it.

Children were just one more thing he didn't have the money for. Pulling a stray hair from his mouth, he lifted her legs from his shoulder and stood.

Betsy lay back on the table, legs splayed, staring at the ceiling and breathing hard.

He couldn't take his eyes off her. "Have you—how do you avoid pregnancy?"

She blinked. "Er." She blinked again, eyes focusing. "There's a woman near town who grows pennyroyal."

"That's for unwanted babes, isn't it?"

She closed her legs then, sitting up and fussing with her skirts. "Not only. If you drink pennyroyal tea before your menses are to start, it helps them on. Too early to call it a babe, or know if there was one."

"Oh." His cock was too hard to waste time in feeling unsettled. "Then may I…?"

Maybe it was rude to ask her that. Maybe he ought to wait for her invitation.

Her glow dimmed further. She chewed at the corner of her mouth. "Yes."

Betsy's body was still slow and warm from pleasure. It was good that he enter her now, when she was wet. She did want this. She'd wanted this for ages.

It just seemed complicated all of a sudden.

But Jemima would go with her to get the pennyroyal, later. She had weeks before her menses were due.

Mr. Moon tucked some hair behind her ear. "Be you certain?"

Oh no. He could see how unsure she was. She didn't want to be a responsibility, or work. She wanted to be effortless and fun. He'd already been so kind to her.

So…magnificently kind. Her body pulsed with heat at the memory.

She smiled up at him, and halfway through the smile it was real. "Yes." She pulled him down to kiss her.

He tasted odd. What—*that's me*, she realized with embarrassment.

But he kissed her eagerly, already fumbling at his breeches. His hands brushed her thighs. He would be *in* her. The magnitude of it amazed her.

"Yes," she said again, almost laughing with joy. "Hurry." He smiled against her mouth.

Abruptly she felt the head of his cock poking at her cunny, round and hard and strange. It jabbed uncomfortably. He jabbed again, searching, and pulled away nervesomely. For a moment she panicked.

But Lenny had found his way in, and he had fit. So would Mr. Moon. "You needn't really hurry," she said. "Sorry."

The tip of his cock slipped in with a bump, and his mouth fell open. His fingertips brushed her folds as he pushed himself into her.

Inch by inch, in he went, and she tried to relax and welcome him, because the look of surprised awe on his face made her want to give him anything, everything. Her heart swelled like rising dough, pressing gently against her ribs trying to get to him.

He thrust hesitantly.

She could feel him inside her, and suddenly that wasn't just a polite way to say she was getting fucked. Inside her body was just herself, had always been just herself, and outside was everything else. But now he was here too. They were joined.

"How does it feel?" she asked shyly.

He grinned at her and thrust harder, somehow making a joke with it, a splendid joke. "I see what all the fuss is about."

She had to swallow a light-headed giggle, of the sort that overtook her and Jemima when they'd stayed awake far too late and everything was suddenly the funniest thing in the world. "Go on, then."

So he took his pleasure—but it didn't feel like taking. He gave her his pleasure without stinting, trusting her to be kind with it.

It wasn't quite comfortable taking him into her, not yet. But it was exciting, and by the time he clutched at her hip with one hand and leaned hard on the table with the other, pounding into her one last time—no, just once more—she was throbbing and eager again.

He rested his forehead on her shoulder a few moments, catching his breath, before standing to button his breeches. "Be you well?"

She nodded, but she was sore and empty, with wetness trickling down her thigh. She hated being awkward and unsure again, when a moment before she had felt her innermost self flowing towards him and gathering him in.

With an effort, she smiled. "I'd better clean up."

When she was done she tossed the rag in with the other kitchen messes. The laundry bucket was growing full; she'd have to wash them all soon.

"Was I—all right?" he asked behind her. "I didn't disappoint you?"

Her heart melted. In just such a voice, a minute or two

from now, he'd ask her to taste the macaroons and reassure him that their texture was even, and that they weren't too sweet.

She didn't want him to know how ready she was to be pleased, how impossible it had been for anything but a refusal to disappoint her.

"You were perfect," she said, trying to sound as if she were merely talking about biscuits. Smoothing her gown over her hips, she let her hands linger on her own curves. He saw her as a woman now. He must. "And…were you pleased?" She couldn't turn and face him.

He chuckled tightly. "When can we do it again?"

She beamed at the bucket of rags. "As soon as you like."

He nudged her gently aside to wash his hands, and by the time she got up the nerve to look at him, he was weighing sugar to be pounded for the Naples biscuits.

The rest of the afternoon passed like any other, except for mirthful, blushing glances and now and again a smothered smile, like two people trying not to laugh in church. Betsy didn't know whether to be relieved that they could still work together or disappointed that everything wasn't changed.

But when the kitchen was lamplit, after he'd washed the dishes and she had scrubbed the floor, he pulled her into the shadows, his hands still damp and rough.

"May I?" he asked, and when she said he might, he lifted her against the wall and took her again. "I'd like you to come while I'm in you," he said earnestly, and she obliged him with very little effort.

She felt very smug indeed as she walked home. She was a seductress.

Betsy Piper, confectioner's shopgirl and seductress. She ought to have cards made up at the printing office.

CHAPTER 3:

Thursday

Betsy let herself into the closed shop with her key, hopeful of a warm welcome but plagued with renewed nerves. Tying her faded green-and-white apron tighter than usual, so it curved closely to her breasts, she ventured into the quiet kitchen, a piece of stale seedcake in hand.

Mr. Moon sat sketching, his free hand fisted in his hair. Head-on, his long nose with a bump in it gave him a coltish, raw-boned, friendly look. But there was something austere in his profile, like a hawk or a monk. Something pure and fierce.

Looking over, he smiled sheepishly, the purity and fierceness out of sight once more. But she knew they were there. "Morning, Betsy. Did you sleep well?"

I dreamed of you, she thought, but she'd never be able to make it sound like a flirtatious joke. It wasn't even true, and he'd believe it.

"I did, thank you. Though I dreamed I was late to work," she said honestly.

"I dreamed all my teeth were falling out one after t'other. I've dreamed that dunnamany times, and I don't know why. I've good teeth and I take care to clean the sugar off." He felt at his jaw as if reassuring himself that his teeth were still firmly in their sockets. "I've made a list of what we'll need to lay the table at the Assembly Rooms. Some things we'll borrow from Mr. Whittle at the Lost Bell, and half a dozen or so I've to beg Mr. Killick for the loan of."

That was the confectioner at Lenfield House. As a boy Mr. Moon had walked there from Runford on his weekly half-holiday, an hour each way, to learn as much as he could from Mr. Killick.

"I need to be getting a start on the gum paste ornaments," he said. "Can I send you to Lenfield? Only a few bitty things will need to be fetched today. I've marked them with an X—a sack or basket ought to suffice."

It was a seven-mile walk, and half an hour after dawn the day was already warm. Betsy tried not to grumble. Someone had to go. "Aye, of course."

He showed her his list, carefully describing each item to her despite the drawings he'd already penciled in the margin. Surely the shop would be a success, soon enough. Surely the love he lavished on it couldn't be wasted.

"You don't mind, do you?"

"Not a jot," she said. "You know I want the assembly to be splendid." She slipped the list into her bodice.

He raised a finger to trace the paper's outline beneath her dress, its flowered print almost invisible with age. "Thanks. I'm sorry, but I think you'd better go before it gets too hot." But he tilted up her chin for a quick kiss. "And there I've got a smudge of lead on you."

He licked his thumb and rubbed it off, and the pink flash of his tongue made even that unromantic gesture unfairly erotic.

The columns for the round temple were crooked.

Robert felt the first cloying tendrils of panic in his nose and throat. Or maybe that was a coating of powdered sugar, from pounding gum dragon and sugar into paste all day.

He'd used this set of dowels a dozen times and never had crooked columns, so he must have coated them unevenly with gum paste. The whole thing would fall the moment someone tried to slice into the blancmange dome on its platter.

Betsy let herself into the kitchen. She looked hot and tired after tramping about under the hot sun all morning; he'd ought to give her a moment to rest.

"The columns are crooked," he said.

Frowning, she set down her basket. "Are they?" Nudging a bucket in front of the door to let in a breeze, she came and stood at his elbow. "Only the smallest bit. Once you've dabbed them with royal icing and stuck the plate on, it should hold."

"Do you think?"

"I do."

Maybe she was right. Maybe a little crookedness could be overlooked. Lively St. Lemeston wasn't London, after all. But he was grateful his old master, Mr. Killick, wouldn't be at the assembly to see it.

"Mrs. Lovejoy came by while you were gone," he said. "She said maybe there'd be two hundred twenty-five at the assembly, and insisted on adding two chocolate cream tarts to the menu. Said it came to her over her morning chocolate."

Betsy rolled her eyes. "Is she paying us extra for them?"

Robert felt ashamed that he wasn't a better negotiator. "She's already paying us such a great sum, and it won't be much extra work, just a little extra tart dough and shaving some chocolate…"

He went and got a platter so he wouldn't have to see Betsy smothering her sigh. It wasn't much use trying to make it balance before everything was pasted in place, but he held it above the columns to see how it would lie.

Mostly flat. Mostly.

"It'll hold," Betsy said firmly. "You'll see. How much more do you have to do?"

"I've made the columns and the steps, but I've still to mold the architrave, frieze, and cornice of the dome, and all the flourishes and ornaments for the frieze."

"The whats of the dome?" She pulled a roll from her basket and dug her thumbs into it to open it. "Would you like one?"

Robert realized that he hadn't eaten since breakfast. "Thank you." He reached for it.

Prying a second one apart, she shook her head and disappeared into the cold room, no doubt for butter and jam.

"Ohhhh," came her voice, loud and soft and loud again as the door swung. "Maybe I won't be right back after all. Latch the door and come in here a moment."

"I should start on the dome."

"Just for a moment," she called. "There are hours and hours of daylight yet."

There were—thank God it was summer—and while Betsy might not be a confectioner she had a good eye and sure hands. She could lay the ornaments on the frieze as neatly as he could. They'd finish the temple by nightfall.

Robert stepped into the cold room, so named because it adjoined the ice room and was away from the heat of the ovens.

Oh. It had been devilish hot in the kitchen, hadn't it? He'd not remarked how much he was sweating until the cool air hit him. He felt calmer and happier at once.

"Did you latch the door?" she asked, and he assured her he had.

They ate companionably, sitting on the edge of an ice chest, and by the time the jammy, buttered roll had gone most of Robert's panic had too.

Snaking an arm around Betsy's waist, he drew her against him. "I'm glad you're back." He caught the edge of a pleased smile as she leaned against his shoulder.

He twisted to kiss her. She kissed him back eagerly, and he thought, *I could have her right now.*

Only moments later, it had become, *I have to have her right now.* "Let's—may I—"

She nodded urgently, her nose bumping against his. One breast was pressed into his side. He'd barely even touched those yesterday. Despite all she had allowed him to do, he still half expected a slap as he put his hands up and shaped them to her curves.

My, but her bosom was soft, softer than the yielding layers of linen that covered it. And there—there were her nipples, stiff beads against his fingers. She gasped and pushed against his hands, reaching under his apron for the buttons on his breeches.

"Not yet," he said. "Let me take your clothes off."

His whole body thrilled as he said the words. There was no confection or fruit the color of her skin, but he thought of delicious things anyway, peach custard and marzipan. That tiny sensitive part of her cunny was the delicate pinkish red of a translucent red-currant ice.

Betsy went stiff. Her nod was very slight.

Had he finally gone too far? Why should *this* be too far?

He took his hands off her and laid them flat on the ice chest. "Do you not want me to?"

She took in a deep breath; he felt a pang of loss at her bodice pushing against air instead of his palms. "Go and check the latch again," she said. "I'll be along in a moment."

He did as she asked, embarrassed in the brightly sunlit kitchen by his obvious erection. Maybe that was how Betsy felt about being naked—afraid of looking foolish. As if she ever could.

Robert laid his apron on the counter. Would it make her less self-conscious if he took off his own clothes, or would it frighten her?

She came in with a blushing smile and a bowl of ice. "You'd ought to take off your clothes too. Would you unlace the back of my gown first?"

"Oh aye," he said eagerly, to make her laugh.

Her stays laced in the front. He'd known that from touching her. He knew dunnamany things about her now that he hadn't known two days ago.

Dunnamany things about her body, anyways.

But he knew her mind well enough already—didn't he? They'd worked together for more than a year now. They'd talked for hours. He knew enough about the last twenty years of Sussex murders that he could write a book, if writing a book were a thing he could do, which it assuredly was not.

He knew about her best friend, Jemima, and her mother's tiresome habit of cooking everything to a mush, and her little sister who wanted to go into service in London but hopefully wouldn't until she was old enough to look out for herself.

He knew Betsy hated peeling apples, that her pattens always gave her a blister the first rainy week of the year, and that the autumn she was ten, she and Jemima had gone nutting every Sunday to see if the devil would really hold down the branches for them as superstition promised.

They stripped in silence. She pulled off her stays, contorting to keep the lace from coming entirely out of its holes, and rolled down her stockings swift and sure as she must do it every night before bed. He watched, and felt he knew her not at all.

What do you lie in the dark and worry over? he wanted to ask her. *How many children do you want, and what sort of old woman would you like to be?*

He couldn't say that. It wasn't bed talk—or kitchen-counter talk, as the case might be.

He took off his own stockings, and his breeches. "Smallclothes too?"

After a pause, she nodded without looking at him.

Robert obeyed, hoping she wasn't disappointed, that his hips weren't too bony and that she wouldn't rather a man have more hair on his chest.

He was the furthest thing from disappointed when she pulled her shift over her head. The curves and angles and textures of her were flawless, all of them. Her golden forearms, neck, and face gave way in stark lines to the pale skin under her dress, inspiring an unexpected tenderness. The sweet curve of her hip and the deep shadows under her breasts made him wild to be in her.

He drew near to her. The possibility of coupling hung in the warm air between them like the smell of something baking in the oven. There were nerves in that too—*will it taste as good as it smells?*—but he was so eager to take the first bite of her, he couldn't pay the nerves much mind.

He could touch any part of her he'd a mind to, could set her up on the counter and slide right in with nothing in the way.

Sweat beaded on her forehead. A drop trailed down her neck and between her breasts, tracing a red crease from a seam of her corset. He licked it up, salt and skin on his tongue, breathing in her heat.

She took a chip of ice from her bowl and ran it across her forehead, down her neck and then—she hesitated ever so slightly—around her left breast. Her lips parted on a sigh.

Robert heaved her onto the counter and spread her thighs, taking himself in hand. She was visibly slick with arousal. He waited for her nod and drove into her at once.

The ice clattered to the floor. She was so hot, the hottest thing in summer, her cunny's grip tight and yielding. He'd ought to pick up the ice before one of them slipped in the puddle, but he felt for it with his foot and kicked it across the kitchen.

He guided her back until she rested on her elbows and he could watch her breasts bounce lewdly and her arse slide on the counter with every thrust. Her head fell back, loose locks of hair swaying. He had never dreamed what this would be like, to see his effect on a woman in that undeniable movement. Already he could feel his pleasure about to peak.

"I'm sorry it's so quick," he got out. "Let me rest a moment, and I'll make it up to you."

She laid a hand flat on his stomach. He was confused at first, and then it struck him that she could feel his muscles tense with each thrust. Her fingers curled a little, and her eyelids drooped in satisfaction.

He spent, watching himself pump helplessly into her until

the pleasure ebbed, and then a little longer. She made a small noise of disappointment when he stopped.

Robert shut his eyes. Her hips filled his hands, her cunt held his cock, but he couldn't see her. He breathed until he felt less wild.

Opening his eyes, he reached for the bowl of ice.

It was hot in the kitchen, and Betsy was sweating with exertion and lust. When Mr. Moon slid a bit of ice along her collarbone, it was a bright pure shock, balanced on the knife-edge between *Please don't* and *Please don't stop*.

The ice slid down her breastbone and made a great swoop over her stomach. She gasped and shivered violently.

She wanted to watch, but it was even better to close her eyes and follow the progress of that patch of cold, now spiraling ever so deliberately up her right breast. She held her breath, bracing herself as he rubbed the ice directly on her nipple. But instead of stinging, it created undiluted sensation, the slippery ice seamlessly arousing every point on her skin one after the other.

His cock was slipping out of her. She wanted him back, or his fingers, or—a piece of ice? Could she bear it?

Suddenly a second piece of ice curled up her right breast. Her nipples were twin points of yearning, stabbing through her, transfixing her. Her hips jerked, and then his hot mouth closed over one icy peak.

She screamed.

He drew back. "Did I—is it not comfortable?"

She squeezed her eyes tighter shut and shook her head,

reaching out blindly. He made a pleased noise, and then there was liquid heat on her breast again.

Mr. Moon's tongue followed ice across her heated skin—arms and hips and inner thighs—hot and cold, soothing and agitating, until she no longer had the strength to do anything but lay on the counter, wood against her back, gasping for breath.

Then, finally, he slid a piece of ice straight down her stomach to where he'd put his mouth yesterday.

That did hurt, the skin there so thin and sensitive that it shrank back desperately. She moaned as icy water dripped down her slit, melted by her heat. Did she want him to stop?

The ice withdrew. She heard it clinking against his teeth, and his knees settling on the floor. She trembled, legs spread wide, until he licked her, his mouth cool and hot by turns.

"Put—put your fingers in me," she begged, tongue clumsy in her mouth.

He slid one in, tentatively, and then another. His fingertips were ice-cold too.

This was the best refuge from summer she'd ever dreamed of. She'd never dreamed anything so glorious.

She remembered suddenly how unsure he always was. She ought to encourage him. But could she really—really *talk* to him while he was licking at her cunny and his fingers were curling deep inside her?

"This is better than eating ices," she said shakily. Her cool breasts basked in the warm air.

He rubbed her with a cold thumb. "Not better than *my* ices, I hope."

She tried to compare, but imagining eating one of his ices, sweet peaches and cream running down her throat—it overwhelmed her. It was too much, too much of him. There was only one thing she wanted to say right now, three short words, and he wouldn't like them. They would sound like a responsibility.

"Nothing's better than your ices," she told him unevenly, since he wanted to hear it. "Your ices make angels covetous."

His fingers twisted. Betsy moaned, pliable in his hands as a bowl of sugar paste. There was no being in this world or the next that wouldn't covet this. She floated, grasping for something solid, and pleasure wrapped its bright wings around her.

Ecstasy drained away, leaving her naked and sweaty on a kitchen counter. She never wanted to move again, but there was work to be done and she must look depraved. Reluctantly, she opened her eyes.

Mr. Moon beamed down at her, running a finger proudly along her hip the way he sometimes did with the cakes when they came out especially puffed and golden. He was naked too, lean and long, and it made her so very happy to sit up and lay her hand on his bare skin, pull him towards her and kiss his shoulder. Happy and afraid.

One week, she'd promised herself. Five days left of it. Could she bear to only have five more days of this?

He liked her, didn't he? Surely a man couldn't make a girl feel this way if he didn't like her dreadfully. He wouldn't look at her like that.

He hesitated, hovering close. Pleasuring her had made him hard again. "May I…? One more time, before we…?"

Betsy nodded, sliding to the edge of the table to welcome him in.

A week couldn't be enough for him either. He'd want forever. He would.

CHAPTER 4 :
Friday

Robert went over his carefully planned schedule again. Today was Friday. If they picked all the berries and made the sugar-of-roses figures for the landscape today, and tomorrow they candied the rose petals…

Betsy came in with her usual cheery greeting. Robert wanted her at once, blood rushing to his cock.

Was it her usual cheery greeting? Or was there something self-conscious in her smile? They had been so comfortable together before.

He smiled back as best he could and bent his head over his list. "We've got to find folk to help us Tuesday. You and me can't possibly churn that many ices ourselves."

"How many sabotieres can we get our hands on?" she asked. Robert only owned two of the small ice makers.

"Five." Even with five, it would be hard to churn enough ice in time, but he could think of nowhere to beg one that he hadn't already begged.

Betsy frowned. He wanted to trace the lovely crease in her forehead with his fingers. "I'll ask Jemima if she can get the afternoon free," she said. "And I think my mother and sister can come. If not, I'll find people."

Robert had come to Lively St. Lemeston for professional reasons: because it was the nearest market town, because it was big enough to support the sort of shop he wanted, because his patroness Lady Tassell had a political interest here and agreed to help him if she could count on his vote when he became a freeman of the borough. But he'd thought it would become home.

Yet after eenamost a year and a half, he had no one here he could ask for help. With the Honey Moon occupying his whole attention, he'd made few friends. *No* friends. Just Betsy.

He supposed the Dymonds were friends after a fashion. But he couldn't bring a woman he'd hoped to marry into the kitchen, now he and Betsy were—entangled. Besides, he already owed the couple far more money than he ever expected to repay.

They didn't expect it either, which was worse. He'd meant their wedding cake to be a gift, and then he'd taken the coins they pressed into his hands, because his credit was running out again with the milkwoman. Every time he saw them he felt ashamed.

He could ask his old friends from Runford to come; it was only a drive of an hour or two. But then they'd see how near he was to failing, after he'd told them all his hopes for the shop.

"Thank you," Robert said gruffly, pulling pails and flat crates from under his worktable. "Did you bring gloves?"

She twisted so he could see them tucked into her apron strings. Despite the heat she wore a long-sleeved dress, old and stained, to ward off raspberry thorns.

He patted his purse nervously. "I've rented a cart, and then we can drive to Wheatcroft and buy our pineapples from his lordship's greenhouse."

Lord Wheatcroft was young and kindhearted and might have let him buy on tick, but the Wheatcrofts were the Tassells' political archrivals, and Robert thought it best not to owe the baron a debt.

This would be the last of his ready money.

"I can't reach!" Betsy complained, laughing. "Ow!"

She was just around a bend in the path, hidden from sight by the same trees and tall raspberry bushes that concealed the River Arun, rushing along a few yards away. Shielding his face, Robert followed her voice around the bend and through a narrow gap in the bushes. He emerged in a small clearing.

The bushes lining the path were picked over, but fat red berries ringed the clearing. Betsy stood on tiptoe, trying to reach a cluster. He plucked them for her, dropping them one by one into her pail.

Taking off his glove, Robert fed her the last one, and then couldn't draw away his hand. Tracing her lower lip, he slid his finger into her mouth.

She closed her lips around it, sucking, and then pulled away with a squeaking little pop. Her tongue was soft.

He wanted to put his cock in her mouth.

Could he ask for that? Had she done it before, with somebody else? This was all a revelation to him, but maybe to her it was nothing out of the common way.

She said bedding you was better than eating ices.

Ices were near a religion to him, but even Robert knew it would be daft to take *that* as any kind of declaration. He fed her another berry.

"Mmm." Her smile was an invitation. "This is a nice spot for our luncheon, don't you think?"

"I—" He flushed. "Yes."

Betsy's eyes sparkled with mischief, as if she knew he'd not been thinking of luncheon. "I'll fetch it from the cart."

She returned with their basket and an ancient bedsheet, which she spread on the ground. "Would you think me very wicked if I took off my bonnet?"

"*Ever* so wicked."

She laughed, setting the bonnet down with her gloves. Dappled sunlight snuggled up to her like a lover, making bright spots in her yellow hair and a sunny circle the size of a farthing on one striped shoulder. He felt suddenly as if touching her wouldn't sate his hunger, any more than eating sweets when you craved salty. He wanted something else from her.

"When we were small I'd take Nan raspberry picking to get her out of Mum's hair. We'd sell the berries to Mrs. Philpotts for jam." Betsy chewed at the corner of her mouth, her smile a little sad. "I always saved a handful for Mum. Sometimes they made her smile."

Robert's hunger was for this, he realized. For her to talk to him. "Was she very sad after your father left?"

She blinked, surprised. "I think he left *because* she was so sad," she said after a moment. "He was a bricklayer, and gone dunnamuch for work, but he was home more before my sister was born. After that…I don't know. I was small. I only know Mum was always crying, and he hated it, and then he was home less. And after a few years of that, he went away for a job and never came back."

She huffed a laugh. "D'you know, I used to think maybe

he'd come back if I made her happy again?"

What a cruel, impossible task for a child. "What would you do if he came back now?" Robert asked. *He* would be tempted to smash the man's face with a rolling pin.

She thought it over, plucking at the edge of the sheet. Her mouth twisted wryly. "He won't."

"Can I ask you a silly question?" His heart pounded.

"Aye, anything," she said, but she looked wary.

"Do you ever—do you ever lie awake at night worrying?"

She laughed. "Doesn't everyone?"

He didn't know. Did they? His face was hotter than the sun or the conversation warranted. "What do you worry over? What are you most afraid of?"

She frowned, dismayed.

She didn't want to tell him. She was glad enough to give him her body, but maybe that was all. There was a lump in Robert's stomach like he'd eaten raw dough.

It was absurd, anyway, to say she gave him her body. No more had she taken his. He'd not mind that, belonging to her. But they were still entirely separate, and could go anywhere they liked, away from each other.

Don't go, he thought. *I'll do anything you like, if you like to ask me for it.*

"Not being good enough," she said, very quiet. "Doing my best and falling short." She laughed. "That and being murdered."

It came so near the endless circle of his own fears that it shocked him. Why should *she* fear? It was plain she was good enough for anything she put her hand to.

It must be a leftover from her childhood and her sad mother, one of those feelings like cheese gone ampery after too long on the shelf. You knew you'd ought to feed it to the pigs but somehow it lurked in the corner for weeks.

All at once he remembered the tight way she'd said, *You were ready enough to take a wife last autumn.*

Did she…did she think herself not good enough for *him*? Did she *want* him to marry her?

Hasty as ever, he'd have liked to propose on the spot. But his debts grew every day. Debtors' prison was…was it likely? It *felt* likely. He didn't want to be another man like her father, abandoning his wife to support a household on her own.

Likely she meant something quite different, anyway.

Betsy lay back and stared blindly at the sky, her face in a patch of sunlight. "Your worst fear is losing the shop, isn't it?"

Panic stirred in his throat.

You're not going to lose the shop, he told himself firmly. *You fret too much, that's all. This assembly will be a roaring success, and Mrs. Lovejoy's twenty-five pounds will pay your debts and give you something to go on.*

Looking at Betsy stretched out on the sheet, he vowed to himself he'd propose when he had those twenty-five pounds in his pocket, and hang the consequences. He couldn't stand not knowing how she felt any longer than that.

Soothed by this promise of relief, he lay down beside her. The sky was bright, bright blue behind the leaves. "I reckon so. You know I'm my parents' only living child."

She rolled towards him, shading her eyes. "Living? Did you have brothers and sisters?"

"They wanted a whacking big brood, but she don't conceive easy, my mother. And then there were two miscarriages and a son and daughter lost to cholera and the influenza, before I was born. They doted on me. I want…I suppose I want to make up for it. To suffice."

"Your mother didn't want you to sell the bakery."

That was an understatement. The bakery had been in his family for generations. It was steady, rock solid. But Robert had never cared about bread. He'd cared about pastry, about fragile, flaking, spun-sugar towers.

"Mum baked us a cake every day for dinner," he said. "To make us happy. To make *me* happy, because I loved sweets. And it did. I want to make people happy."

"I know."

He'd told her this before, but he didn't think he'd ever made her understand how *much* he wanted it. "Mrs. Lovejoy told me sometimes she can't hear herself think, but when she comes into the Honey Moon, she can breathe again. I want the shop to be that, in folks' lives. A slice of joy, a morsel of calm when they've need of it. A place that won't ever turn them away."

Robert could see it so clearly in his mind. He'd staked everything on it, and if he failed, then he'd sold lifetimes of sober hard work for naught. He'd been entrusted with his parents' hopes, and willfully dashed them.

"So long as they have extra pennies in their pocket." Betsy sighed. "I'm sorry, that was mean. I don't know what's got into me."

The words pierced him. She was right, sugar and cream weren't cheap. It would have been wiser, and more virtuous, to keep to the honest labor of flour and water and yeast.

"I thought…" He was almost afraid to say it. "I thought you liked the shop."

"Of course I do," she said at once, warmly. "I'm sorry I'm being so dull."

He felt across the sheet until his hand found hers. "I don't mind." He brought her hand up—would she think him strange?—and kissed the back of it. "You're cheerful to everyone. I'm glad you know you can be dull with me."

She took in a sharp breath, as if he'd hurt her.

When he glanced over in surprise, she was blinking furiously. "Thank you," she said thickly.

Don't cry, he wanted to say, and *Please don't be unhappy*. But he'd just said she could.

He rolled towards her, covering her body with his. *I'm unhappy too.* He kissed her as if his mouth could communicate the thought without words.

Her fingers curved around his skull. It filled him with such violent yearning he couldn't breathe. He wanted to swallow the small hungry sound she made, wanted to dissolve into her the way sugar dissolved into water and was neither sugar nor water, but something new.

She wanted to be good enough, and he'd never even told her how wonderful she was out loud.

He kissed the curve of her cheek and along her jaw, downy as a peach. "You're beautiful," he said before he could think better of it, and kissed her neck so she'd not see him waiting for her reaction.

She sucked in a breath. For the compliment, or the kiss? He shaped her body with his palm. "You're like—"

Oh Lord, he couldn't say she was like a sweet-smelling lump of dough, round and soft and full of promise. He couldn't say she was like honey on his tongue. He had thoughts that weren't about the kitchen, didn't he?

"Like—"

She went perfectly still. He could feel her listening even

when he curled his hand where her buttock rolled into her thigh, his fingertips inches from her cunt. Her breath stuttered hopefully.

"Like summer," he said, pleased with the thought, and she sighed in satisfaction. "When the trees are laden with fruit and everything is warm and growing."

"There really is something wanton about summer, isn't there?" Her voice was lazy and content.

He took hold of her hips and rolled them until he lay on his back, Betsy sprawled atop him. She sat up, a leg to either side of him, looking a trifle dizzy and perplexed. Mmm, he liked that. He could see all of her. "Beautiful."

She blushed and smiled. Her hair was tumbling down, on the side. "Should we, outdoors?"

"We'd hear someone coming." He twisted that loose hair around his finger. "So soft."

It was a miracle, the way she looked. There was more architectural mastery in the tilt of her nose than any half a dozen cathedrals one cared to name.

Would she be charmed if he said that? Or would it sound pompous, as if he were trying to be poetic when he was only a confectioner? He'd never even seen a cathedral, only engravings of them in a textbook.

He tugged at her skirts, and she rose up on her knees to gather them out of the way while he unbuttoned his breeches.

"You…" she said hesitantly.

Oh God, what? He held his breath.

"You're quite handsome yourself." Her smile was half sly and half self-conscious.

Somehow it didn't matter that he'd already known she must think so. He puffed up like a soufflé.

She took his cock in her hand. "And your proportions are very good."

Ohh, she drove him wild. He'd asked her that dunnamany times about a sugar sculpture: *Are the proportions tolerable?*

Her mouth curved as she frigged him. "You like that, don't you?"

He grunted and thrust into her fist, unable to think of a clever answer. She filled his vision, stray bits of raspberry bush and sky around the edges of her.

"I love your eyes," he told her.

"You do?" she said, sounding surprised and flattered, and shut them. "What color are they?"

Did she really think he didn't know? "Green with honey in the center."

She opened them, blinking. "I always thought of them as hazel."

"Same thing."

"I like your nose," she offered shyly, even as her hand tugged familiarly at his cock.

His fingers dug into her thighs. His nose? But it was enormous and lumpy.

"It's so friendly from the front, and so severe from the side."

"Please," he got out. "Please."

"Do you want something?" she teased.

He remembered that he did. "Would you…"

"Mmm?"

"…put your mouth on it?"

Her hand stopped. Betsy looked down, scrunching up just the left side of her face. "I…" She licked her lips uncertainly and his cock jumped in her hand.

She laughed. "Why not, I suppose." She rustled away down his legs, and he almost changed his mind with wanting her back.

She leaned forward, her mouth inches from his cock poking through her fist. "It looks like we'll be getting better acquainted," she told it.

He flexed his hips so it bobbed a greeting. Speaking for it in a little high voice seemed like too much, but the idea made him swallow a laugh.

Her lips brushed him, feather light, and then she closed them around the head of his cock.

Oh. *Oh.* He hadn't thought it would feel *that* good. He hadn't thought it would be quite so overwhelming to see her bent over him, eyes closed and mouth around the most sensitive part of him. Taking him in. Tasting him. Her hair tickling the soft skin at the crease of his thigh.

She hesitated, and then her tongue licked at him.

His hips jerked upwards, and she choked.

"Sorry," he said hoarsely, holding very still. After a moment she bobbed her head. *Oh Lord.*

That was blasphemy, wasn't it? But this felt like prayer, it did—this immense silent asking and hoping in his chest. *Please, God, let me be this happy.*

"You're so beautiful." He repeated it until he didn't know what he was saying, only that he meant it more than he'd ever meant anything in his life. *Beautiful, beautiful, beautiful*, with each wet slide of her mouth over his skin, his hands fisted in the sheet.

She went slow and so careful and that was good, like taking small bites of cake to make it last longer, he didn't want this ever to end.

"I'm going to—"

But she didn't stop. Instead she tightened her mouth around him and sucked. Her teeth scraped him clumsily, and somehow that was what made him spend.

She sputtered a little, and distantly he thought, *I should stop shaking,* but he couldn't.

When it was over, he lay like a beached fish, gasping. He'd been terribly selfish. He'd spilled his seed in her *mouth.*

She swallowed, making a face, and reached for the flask of lemonade.

"Kiss me first," he blurted out. "If you don't mind."

She grimaced, but she did it. When he slipped his tongue between her lips she mostly tasted like Betsy and her lunch, but a faint flavor lingered, salty and earthy like mushrooms.

He'd spilled his seed in her mouth, and she'd swallowed it. "Thank you."

"You're welcome. Do you think you might return the favor?"

"I can think of nothing I'd like better," he told her honestly.

When they got back to the bakery, Mrs. Lovejoy was knocking on the kitchen door.

"Oh, there you are!" she said with brittle gaiety. There were dark circles under her eyes. "Do you think we might have some fresh figs? They're Sir William's favorite."

Still warm and relaxed from their day in the sun, Robert laughed. He didn't mean it in an ill-natured way, but he saw Mrs. Lovejoy stiffen.

"I beg your pardon, ma'am." He couldn't quite stop smiling

yet. He even felt in charity with Mrs. Lovejoy, since her money would let him propose to Betsy. "Figs are out of season another month at least."

"Green figs, then."

"I haven't any on hand and they take weeks to make."

By the time she left, Robert had agreed to a little tree for the temple lawn hung with candied figs from the jar in the cold room, and his smile had long gone.

CHAPTER 5 :
Saturday

When Betsy let herself into the kitchen, Mr. Moon was already kneading dough for brown bread ice cream, sleeves rolled above his elbows. He gave her a shy smile, and it occurred to her that now she might tell him something.

"I like watching you knead dough," she confessed.

His forehead creased. "You do?" Tendons shifted in his forearms, the strength and dexterity of his hands terribly evident.

She nodded. "It displays your arms to great advantage."

He ducked his head, ears going red, but his mouth curved. "Does it now?"

A brand-new thought occurred to her. "I—" How bold was too bold? "You wouldn't—you wouldn't consider taking your shirt off to do it, would you?"

He blinked. "I can't see no harm in it, I suppose."

Watching him unknot his apron ties and unbutton his waistcoat, with a few bashful glances in her direction, was as good for thrills and suspense as the transcript of a really good murder trial. Better, maybe. She held her breath.

Slipping his braces back over his shoulders, Robert retied his apron and resumed kneading. Now she could see the muscles in his upper arms and shoulders too. Her mouth watered.

"If I'm to do this," he said, "then you'd ought to work in your shift."

The idea was terribly shocking, and she loved it at once. She winked at him, straining behind her head for the buttons on her dress. She winked! *Betsy Piper, shopgirl and seductress.*

Soon there was nothing but shift and apron between her and his eyes. Her first thought was how cool it was, and how unfair to be obliged to wear stays, a petticoat, *and* a dress in the heat of summer.

Her second thought was that her shift was threadbare with washing and patched under one arm. She was poor, which was why he wouldn't think of marrying her. Maybe she hadn't ought to remind him.

Then she saw he was hard, and thoughts fled. Yet he made no move towards her, but smiled, continuing to work his dough.

Oh. She flamed up like a fire splashed with brandy. They were to go about their business, then. Behave as if it were any day, with both of them half-naked and his cock poking his apron into a fine awning.

She couldn't have said why the idea worked on her so, but her cunny was so eager it hurt.

"Now," he said, "to candy rose petals…"

Betsy was laying out the last of the rose petals when, without warning, Mr. Moon pressed up against her back and murmured in her ear, "Time for our elevener."

He'd been patient all morning, contenting himself with watching her, brushing up against her, fondling her once or twice on his way past. She'd trailed her fingers across his shoulders, leaned over to show him her tits—how unthinkably awkward that had seemed when Jemima mentioned it a few days ago!—and discovered a fondness for slapping his bum.

Neither of them were in much mood to be patient any longer.

He kissed her shoulder, sucking gently and then hard until tingling pressure built at the spot. He drew her arse against his hardness with a hopeful little moan. "May I?"

Please. "Yes. You don't—it's kind of you to ask, but you needn't—"

She felt him tense. He probably thought it a criticism, he was that conscious of his inexperience, thinking her some sort of woman of the world. She'd have to own up about that one of these days.

"I love that you ask," she said. "You're not obliged to, is all I mean. You can—you can have me whenever you like."

Then she wished she hadn't said it. It was too close to the truth. It *was* the truth. He could have her whenever he liked, all of her, to be his wife, and yet he didn't take her. But he was eager enough for *this*, wasn't he?

Maybe he thought *anyone* could have her whenever he liked.

A man don't shit in his hat and put it on his head, her mother's voice said. Not talking about good little Betsy, oh no. Talking about Jemima, whom Mrs. Piper was convinced was the Scarlet Woman of West Sussex.

Jemima might have kissed more boys than Betsy had

fingers and toes, but she'd never behaved as shamelessly, as recklessly, as Betsy was doing now.

Mr. Moon pulled up her shift with an approving sound, squeezing her buttocks. Fire and longing laced through her.

Sliding the tray of rose petals aside, she bent over the table as he lifted her up and took her. Her feet dangled helplessly; he was so tall. So tall and perfect.

Her breasts pressed against the smooth marble slab, cool even in summer. Its unforgiving edge cut into her upper thighs, but his cock made her forget it, made the discomfort a token of his hunger for her.

His fingers landed on the back of her neck lightly enough to tickle. He went slower now. Sliding his hand into her hair, he cupped her skull gently but firmly, holding her there for him to fuck. She pressed her forehead into her folded arms and tried not to cry.

"I'd like to decorate your breasts," he said idly. "With rose petals, and a raspberry to cover each nipple."

Why say something so foolish? Candied rose petals were too dear and too laborious to waste on something like that, and they both knew it. She might as well say she'd like to see him dressed for dinner at Lenfield House.

"Betsy?" He smoothed her back uncertainly. "Be you well? Did I—?"

Her shoulders had gone tense, she realized. She nodded hastily.

"I didn't mean to knabble on. I'll hold my tongue."

That wasn't what she wanted at all, but anything she said now would come out sullen, and she couldn't explain her mood.

"Harder," she said, surprising herself.

He put his hands on her hips first, inserting his fingers between that hard marble edge and her skin. He was so awfully, horribly sweet even as he took her with punishing strokes, grunting with effort. How dare he be so sweet?

"Is that—?" He cut himself off, and she knew he'd meant to ask if that was hard enough.

She wished he would just pound into her, heedless. She wanted this to feel angry, so she could feel angry back.

Would you marry me if I were rich? she'd ask spitefully, only to feel his rhythm falter.

She knew the answer already. Aye, he would. He'd been ready to marry Phoebe Dymond, whom he didn't care a pin for, whose blazing rows with her late husband were legend in Lively St. Lemeston, who didn't even like *cake*, because she'd have come with money. It had been the widow, not Mr. Moon, who got cold feet.

Mr. Moon would probably have been too softhearted even to row with her; she'd have browbeaten him entirely.

He'd never told *her* he wanted to decorate her breasts with rose petals. Betsy had had to remind him to pay her the mildest of compliments.

Betsy had done that for him, because she loved him. She'd chosen his happiness over hers, and he'd chosen the Honey Moon over his own happiness. What was *wrong* with them?

His fierce thrusts almost satisfied the violent heat inside her, her sudden hatred of him and herself.

Would he have taken Mrs. Dymond like this? Would he have liked it?

She imagined it: Mrs. Dymond's hands on him. His moans in her ear at this moment.

A wave of possessiveness rolled over Betsy until she

choked on it, her skin tingling with rage, blood rushing to the surface. *Mine.*

"Touch me," she said fiercely. "Make me spend." She was tired of being wholesome and cheerful. She wanted to *kill* something.

The fingers of one hand flexed on her hip. He made a strangled noise, too far gone to obey.

She couldn't reach to do it herself at this angle. She pushed herself up on her elbows and rubbed clumsily at her own nipples. Pleasure speared through her, but not enough.

He shuddered convulsively, spilling into her. Of course. He was satisfied, and she was left wanting.

Someone knocked hard on the door to the kitchen.

Betsy's heart, already pounding, began to hammer violently in her chest.

"Mr. Moon?" There was no mistaking those apologetically petulant tones. Mrs. Lovejoy.

Mr. Moon pulled swiftly out of her, and by the time she pushed herself up, he was pulling off his apron. Light poured over his bare chest lovingly as syrup, dripping down the lean lines of his ribs and stomach. Of course it did. Betsy wanted to hit him.

She ran for her clothes.

"Just a moment, Mrs. Lovejoy," he called, pulling his shirt on. He had so many less clothes than she—and more presence of mind, because he held the door to the cold room open for her.

She gathered up her stays, her petticoats, her dress, her shoes. Had she missed anything? Had she left any telltale sign of her presence, like a bloody knife dropped by a murderer? She felt like a murderer, guilty and creeping, fear driving out rage and leaving her appalled at herself.

She scurried into the cold room and crouched there, afraid even to dress. Her skin broke out in gooseflesh.

I deserve this, she thought.

She wasn't even sure what crime this corrosive guilt was for. Fornication? Wrath? Not being the perfect mistress?

Mr. Moon opened the kitchen door. "How do you do, ma'am?"

"Oh, you know." Mrs. Lovejoy gave a little laugh. If Betsy had to turn that laugh into words, they'd be, *I know you understand how brave I am in the face of my life's many trials.* The woman didn't ask how *he* did. "I wanted to see how things are coming for the assembly. No one answered at the front door."

Betsy hadn't heard her knocking. They had been making too much noise.

"I didn't hear you." He was still breathing hard, and probably blushing like mad. If Mrs. Lovejoy guessed…

"Absorbed in your work, I'm sure," she said with another little laugh, this one playful. Betsy ground her teeth. Oh, she would be here all morning. "May I see what you've done?"

"I'm just candying rose petals today. Wait here, if you please, I'll fetch out the temple."

Betsy shrank deeper into her corner as he came through the door, pulling it carefully shut behind him and crossing to where the sugar sculpture stood on an ice chest. In this moment, she could think of nothing but how foolish she must look. Her nose was running in the chilly air. If she were really a woman of the world, would she know how to think this all a very fine joke?

Going back out, he did his best to shut the door quickly with his arms full, but it swung a little.

If they were caught, he'd *have* to marry her—and then she'd lose her chance at ever knowing he'd chosen her freely, because he adored her, just as she was. She shut her eyes so Mrs. Lovejoy couldn't see her, like a child hiding from bugbears.

"Do you think an Egyptian temple would be better?" Mrs. Lovejoy asked. "After all, the Battle of the Nile was in Egypt."

A sob rose in Betsy's throat. Nothing was ever good enough. Nothing.

That temple was loving, precise, *beautiful* work. Mr. Moon had labored for hours over it, and Mrs. Lovejoy didn't have even one nice thing to say. He would break his heart. He only wanted to make people happy.

Other people.

There was a long, horrified silence in kitchen. "I'm afraid it's too late to make the change," Mr. Moon said apologetically. "We did agree on Grecian. Next year, if you like?"

Another long pause. "Next year, then. And how do you intend to decorate it?"

Betsy shivered through long minutes of "Do you think meringue might be nicer?" and "There *will* be sugar paste men and women, won't there?" and "I do love raspberries…" How Mrs. Lovejoy contrived to have so many opinions and yet be so indecisive was a true mystery.

She ought to be wasting *Betsy's* time. That was Betsy's work, so Mr. Moon could do his own.

"Can you put some of the jellies in martial molds? Cannons and so on?"

"I'm afraid I haven't any," Mr. Moon said. His pained pauses got less and less with each question, at least. "And I don't know anyone who does."

"Could you have one made?"

"Not by Tuesday," he said firmly.

"Then perhaps Lord Wellington's new coat of arms might be displayed somewhere."

Betsy sank down to the floor, pressing her chest and forearms against her thighs for a little warmth, and tried not to imagine murdering her.

"Have you a picture?" Mr. Moon asked. "I can't send to London by Tuesday."

"There was one in the *Intelligencer* when his lordship was made a Knight of the Garter," Mrs. Lovejoy said eagerly. "When was that? Before Vitoria, I know…February?"

"I'll send Betsy to the printing office," he agreed. "If Jack Sparks can find it, I'll paint the arms on a sheet of gum paste for the table."

"Where is that girl? Shouldn't she be helping you?"

Betsy stopped breathing.

"I sent her out on an errand."

"Dawdling somewhere flirting, I don't doubt." Mrs. Lovejoy sighed so loudly it was audible in the cold room. "She has an eye for the men, I've noticed."

Betsy's jaw dropped. *What?*

"I've always found her a very modest young woman," Mr. Moon said, without a trace of self-consciousness at the lie.

"Oh, well, I'm sure she's careful when she knows you're watching."

She glared at the door. But inwardly, her blood ran colder. What if he believed Mrs. Lovejoy?

"I'm afraid I've a deal more to get done today. I assure you, ma'am, that everything will be ready for Tuesday, and to your satisfaction." Mr. Moon sounded annoyed. Could he be jealous? Jemima would call jealousy a good sign, but Betsy felt faintly ill at the thought.

"I'm sorry, you must be wishing me at Jericho," Mrs. Lovejoy said with a mortified little laugh.

"Not at all, ma'am."

"You're too kind, I know you must be bored to death of me."

And still it was minutes more before the bolt finally slid home behind her. Betsy stood, limbs stiff, and walked out into the warmth of the kitchen.

"Are you all right?" he asked.

"Of course." She smiled tightly as she yanked her shift over her head.

"You never—you never spent. Shall I—?"

She drew back.

He saw it. Miserably, he turned away and went to stand in front of his temple.

"You can't please everybody," she said, and wished there wasn't an edge in her voice.

He measured the columns with his hands. "I can't please anybody."

"What she said," Betsy said with sudden resolve, "about me flirting—"

He didn't look at her, but he turned his head slightly in her direction so that she saw him in profile, fierce and austere.

She faltered. "I…"

"I hope someday I shall have the right to ask you what you do when you aren't with me," he said quietly. "But I don't. I know that well enough. And I know you aren't—" He took a deep breath. "You're always quite prompt on errands."

As if that was the point.

Suddenly she couldn't bear to admit that the last man

who'd bedded her was fifteen-year-old Lenny Sadler. That she'd been waiting about for Mr. Moon, dreaming of him, longing for him.

It would only make him nervous, anyway. She couldn't bear that humiliation on top of everything else.

CHAPTER 6:
Sunday

B etsy did not love Sunday mornings. It might be called a day of rest, but she couldn't even sleep late, because she had to get up and put on her Sunday best. She had to cram herself into the gallery at St. Leonard's, everyone shoving and elbowing to the front so they could show the whole church how respectably they were dressed, and then she had to stand through a long sermon.

She didn't mind the sermon. It was the standing she hated, after a long week on her feet. Mrs. Piper was even shorter than Betsy, and liked to be early to claim a coveted spot crushed against the railing. Betsy spent most Sunday mornings gazing enviously down into the box pews with their benches and cushions.

Sunday afternoons, on the other hand, were usually delightful.

But today everything was backwards. After church Betsy had to hurry back to the Honey Moon instead of lazing about with Jemima, and she was eager to get to St. Leonard's and maybe smile at Mr. Moon to make up for yesterday's ill humor.

"Does my hair look all right?" she asked Nan. Their small

mirror showed only a few square inches of it at a time, and that distorted.

"What difference can it make?" Nan said. "It'll be under your hat."

Betsy sighed, wishing she'd saved her money for that bonnet she'd been eying in Miss Tice's window, even if Miss Tice was a Tory. It had paper honeysuckle climbing in thick clusters over the hatband and was the prettiest thing Betsy had ever seen.

Of course she spent her spare coins on sweets and coffee as fast as she earned them, instead.

Still, she felt pleased with her appearance. Her dark purple Sunday dress had faded to a lovely shade of lilac, and her kerchief and gloves had no stains even if they weren't really *white* any longer. Her bonnet had a new ribbon and she'd bought lovely paste shoe buckles from a peddler at the market, which winked as she walked in a very gratifying way.

"I don't know why you bother," Nan said. "He's always late to church and never stands with us."

Betsy flushed hot.

But he'd said *I hope someday I shall have the right to ask you what you do when you aren't with me.* That had to mean marriage. Maybe…maybe today would be different.

Or maybe he'd be so shamed by what they'd been doing that he'd not come to church at all.

But when the Pipers climbed the stairs to the still nearly empty west gallery, Mr. Moon was waiting by one of the arches, in the center just behind the pulpit. Mrs. Piper's favorite spot.

Betsy's heart skipped a beat. Today was different after all!

He gulped and straightened when he saw them, turning his battered tricorne round in his hands. Oh, he was so very handsome! When he smiled, nervous but genuine, her heart pounded like a mortar in a pestle.

She hadn't ought to think of bed in church, but how could she help it? Those long fingers white on the brim of his hat had…

She swallowed hard herself, trying to forget. "How lovely to see you! Mama, you know Mr. Moon."

"Of course. How nice to see you again." Mrs. Piper chatted pleasantly while Betsy tried to contain the happiness bubbling up inside her. Even seeing Mrs. Dymond fussing over her sister's new son in their pew near the back of the church barely dampened her mood.

"Did you hear the baby was born two months early?" Nan whispered. "That means she was pregnant during the election. Do you suppose that had anything to do with why her sister tried to marry Mr. Moon? I'm glad the father did the right thing in the end."

"Do you think Mr. Gilchrist *is* the father?" Betsy whispered back.

Mrs. Dymond's brother-in-law lifted the boy above his head to play birdie with every evidence of joyful adoration. "Oh, look at him," said Nan. "He must be."

Betsy bit her lip. Mr. Piper had been Nan's undisputed father, but Betsy couldn't remember him ever holding her like that.

"Girls, don't gossip in church," Mrs. Piper said.

Betsy raised her eyebrows at her. "You just wish you could hear what we're saying."

Mrs. Piper laughed. "I can guess, and so would they if they looked your way. Leave that child be."

Looking up at his nephew, Mr. Dymond caught sight of

them and waved. Mr. Moon waved back, so he was looking at them too.

Betsy's hopeful mood crumpled.

She was swept with bitter envy at Mrs. Dymond's family pew. *Her* father had been a lawyer, practically a gentleman. Standing up with the Pipers, was Mr. Moon thinking he'd have not one, but three new poor female dependents if he married Betsy?

"I owe them so much money, and they've barely got any themselves." He beat a nervous tattoo on his hat brim. "She looks happy, though, don't she?"

Just at the moment, Mrs. Dymond was grumping with Jack Sparks about something or other that made them both very indignant, but Betsy knew what Mr. Moon meant. She nodded wordlessly.

He laughed a little. "Happier than she'd have been with me, I don't doubt."

"Nick Dymond looks happier than you'd have been with her too." Oh, of all the shrewish things to say! When she'd meant to be so cheerful.

"I'm glad," Mr. Moon said. "He were miserable last fall."

She felt more ashamed than ever. Robert Moon was sweet as ice cream, and she kept acting like curdled milk.

Robert chewed over that comment of Betsy's all through the service. Would he have been happy with Mrs. Dymond? He'd been so afraid of losing the Honey Moon that he'd barely thought about it. He'd *never* thought about it. He'd thought only that he'd never be happy again if he let the shop fail.

He was happy with Betsy. He was happy just standing next to her looking down at a hole in the top of her bonnet. He could hear her voice in among everyone else's during the responses, soaring shyly during the hymn.

She sang a little off-key. It charmed him terribly. He couldn't wrap his mind around the idea that this first bloom of love might ever wear off and one day, as a middle-aged man, he might now and again be irritated by it.

Again he promised himself that as soon as he had his twenty-five pounds in hand, he'd ask her to marry him.

He'd always meant to wait until the Honey Moon regularly turned a profit. But if Mrs. Dymond was happy broke, Betsy could be too, and it was only for a little while, wasn't it? The shop was doing better now than last year. Next year it would do better still, and one day, he'd pay the Dymonds back and have enough left over to buy Betsy as many new hats as she liked.

Coming out of church, Robert spied their milkwoman. "Good morning, Mr. Diplock, Mrs. Diplock, how do you do? I'm glad I ran into you, ma'am. I just wanted to be sure you'll have those twenty gallons of cream for me tomorrow morning."

She chewed at her lip. "Mr. Moon, might I speak to you apart a moment?"

Mr. Diplock made a worried face. "Oh, Bell, don't, it's Sunday."

She gestured helplessly. "He asked me on Sunday."

Robert's heart sank. "What is it, ma'am?"

"It's a business matter, sir. Maybe…" She looked at Betsy.

He knew it would be bad news. He'd have liked to tell Betsy to wait a little ways off. It would all come right in the end and it was no use her worrying over it. Faith, he could do *that* enough for both of them.

Or maybe it wouldn't come right. Maybe Mrs. Diplock wouldn't give him the cream for the assembly, and he'd never get that twenty-five pounds. Robert's heart raced.

Betsy glanced up at him, the uneasy tilt of her mouth and one uncertain eye all he could see below the brim of her bonnet. His arm was sweating where she held it, and her skirts were worse than a woolen blanket against his leg. But he didn't want her any farther away.

He was going to make her his wife. He *was*. A man hadn't ought to hide things from his wife. And she'd a way of calming him down when he fretted.

"That's all right, Mrs. Diplock. What is it?"

"Do you know how many gallons of milk have to be skimmed to make that much cream?"

He did, and the figure was so high he couldn't bring himself to say it. "Not—not to the gallon, ma'am. But I know it's a good many." *That's why it costs so damn much*, he added silently.

"A good many indeed." She sighed. "I'll have it for you, Mr. Moon. I've sorted it out with the dairies already. But after that, there'll be no more milk or cream or butter on credit until I'm paid in full what you owe me. And after that, I'll expect you to settle up every fortnight, rain or shine. I've got my own family to think of."

Her husband looked very embarrassed, but Robert sagged with relief. She was giving him the cream. "Of course, Mrs.

Diplock. That's no more or less than fair. Thank you. You've been very patient, and I'm that grateful."

"You needn't worry," Betsy said cheerfully. "When he's paid for the assembly, he'll have the money."

His hopes felt less flimsy, to hear her echo them. Robert took a long, steadying breath.

The milkwoman sighed again. "I hope so, Miss Piper. I do hope so."

When they were almost past the churchyard, Betsy said timidly, "I wouldn't…I wouldn't mind dealing with some of the tradespeople. If you wanted me to. Since you…"

Since it makes you wriggle like a hooked worm. She was too kind to say it, but shame ate at him, sharp as vinegar. "I hadn't ought to get so wrought up about it. It doesn't help anything."

She leaned her head on his arm, just for a moment. "It's harder to change how you feel than it is to change who talks to the milkwoman." There was a little silence. "I'm sorry. It's none of my business."

"No, it is," he said. "I…" But he couldn't finish the sentence, even though she looked pleased by it. He meant to make all his business her business, and what shabby business it was!

She would calm him when he fretted, and take on responsibility for his debts, and talk to the tradespeople and make him eat breakfast when he'd forgot to, and what would he give her, exactly? Would he ever really be able to buy her those hats?

What if her mother had to go on the parish one day because he hadn't provided?

Luckily, she was distracted by her friend Jemima rushing up. "Richard Ralph was found not guilty."

Betsy's jaw dropped. "No."

Jemima was frowning even more deeply than usual. "The

defense managed to convince those fools that his wife might have died of an apoplexy."

A great deal of heated chatter about witnesses, surgeons, and blood followed, which left Robert not much to do except feel vaguely unsettled at how many murders seemed to go on all the time, and specifically unsettled about his finances.

A gaily unhappy voice stopped him in his tracks. "Mr. Moon! Were you going to go by without saying good morning?"

He tried to smile. Betsy and Jemima went quiet as mice. "Good morning, Mrs. Lovejoy. I'm sorry, I didn't see you."

Her eyes narrowed. "You weren't avoiding me, were you?"

"Of course he was avoiding you," her husband said with a snort. "He looks like a man with somewhere to be and no time to listen to you jabber."

Mrs. Lovejoy flushed bright red.

Robert's skin crawled with sympathetic humiliation. "I promise I wasn't avoiding you, ma'am. I was only lost in thought. We're on our way now to juice the pineapples for your ices."

"But it's the day of rest!"

That brought Robert up short. They *had* to work today, or they wouldn't be done in time. What should he say?

Mr. Lovejoy snorted again, trying to meet Robert's eye in a hearty man-to-man way, which didn't help. Urgency filled up his brain, pushing out all the words.

"We haven't that much to do, Mrs. Lovejoy," Betsy said brightly. "We'll rest as soon as we're able. I feel rested enough for a week already, though. Wasn't it an uplifting sermon?"

Mrs. Lovejoy glared at her. "Don't take that flippant tone with me, young woman. You're always *so* polite to everyone else. Isn't my money as good as theirs?"

Betsy's hand tightened on his arm. Robert hoped very

much that Jemima wouldn't say anything cutting. For the moment, she merely kept her stony gaze fixed on Mrs. Lovejoy in what Robert knew was silent condemnation, but to strangers might be indistinguishable from indifference.

Mr. Lovejoy rolled his eyes. "Christ, not this again."

Mrs. Lovejoy flinched. "Don't you take the Lord's name in vain," she said without conviction.

Robert felt a headache coming on. "She wasn't being flippant, ma'am."

"I meant no disrespect," Betsy said nervously. "I swear I didn't, ma'am. I'm that sorry if I seemed flippant."

Mrs. Lovejoy ignored her, her face softening as she looked at Robert. "Oh, you always see the best in people, don't you? That reminds me, do you think we could have a few bowls of pastilles and candies scattered—"

"You're embarrassing yourself. Let's leave these people to their business." Mr. Lovejoy stalked off, leaving his wife alone.

The three members of the lower orders stared at their feet, unwilling to say anything that might make matters even worse.

Mrs. Lovejoy drew herself up. "I accept your apology, Betsy. I suppose you don't know any better. You ought to improve your mind instead of reading about those grisly crimes." Betsy stiffened and Jemima audibly set her teeth. "I've got a book of sermons, really edifying ones, that I think would help you to lift yourself up a little. I'll bring it with me next time I come to the shop."

It was so unfair when Betsy had spent dunnamany hours of her life being kind to Mrs. Lovejoy! "Thank you, ma'am, but please don't," Robert said.

But Betsy murmured, "It's very good of you to take the trouble, ma'am. I'd be that grateful. Thank you."

Mrs. Lovejoy hesitated for a moment, glancing after her husband. Then she nodded regally, bid them good day, and swept off.

Robert offered up a silent prayer of thanks for her forgetting about the bowls of pastilles and candies. A Sunday miracle, that was. Did she think sugar was free?

"What an awful man," Betsy said.

"She's worse," Jemima opined. "Not that that would be an excuse if he strangled her."

Betsy gave a nervous bark of laughter. "Oh, well," she said noncommittally. "I'll talk to you later, Jemima, all right? Maybe we can find a transcript."

Jemima hugged her, nodded at Robert with a look he was painfully aware was also silent condemnation, and stalked off.

Betsy sighed. "I didn't sound flippant, did I?"

"No."

"I should have stopped my clapper. I'm such a busybody."

Robert felt low as dirt. "Please don't," he said. "It wasn't your fault. I couldn't think of a thing to say."

"I don't know what I ever did to make her dislike me."

"Oh, she's just particular." He couldn't quite voice his suspicion that Mrs. Lovejoy disliked Betsy precisely because he, Robert, liked her. It would sound like puffing himself up, and maybe Betsy would laugh and tell him he flattered himself.

The Lovejoys were still visible on the path ahead of them, the husband violently shaking his wife's hand off his arm. Betsy shook her head. "Jemima's right. It don't end well, staying with a man like that. She'd ought to leave him."

He blinked. "Maybe you *have* been reading about too many murders."

She pursed her lips. "Maybe. But when a woman's

murdered, half the time it's her husband." Her bonnet tilted slightly in his direction. "Or her lover. Read the papers if you don't believe me."

"I'm not going to murder you!"

She sighed. "I *know* that."

He hadn't been her first lover. Was he her only lover now? When would she have time for another? "There isn't—there isn't anyone you are afraid of, is there?"

What would Robert do if there was? He'd never been one for fights, but he supposed he'd have to protect her. He'd sort it out. He'd talk to Lady Tassell, if he had to.

She didn't answer right away. They reached the Honey Moon, and he let them into the kitchen.

"Lock it behind you," she reminded him. She hung her bonnet on the peg, and stood there smoothing the ribbons for long moments before turning to face him.

"Please don't be angry with me. I—I didn't lie! You weren't my first. But my first was a long time ago. And you *are*, well, you're my second. I'm not really any kind of woman of the world."

For a moment he was glad. This must mean something then, mustn't it?

Maybe she'd only been satisfied with him because she hadn't anything to compare him to, after all.

"I didn't want you to feel obliged to marry me," she said in a very small voice. "I wanted this to be fun."

"What does that mean?" he demanded, startled by his own sudden anger. She'd let him think things were one way, and they were another entirely. What was she about? Why resist temptation so long and then give in, if not because you wanted *more* than just fun? "Would you even marry me if I asked you?"

She glared back. "Are you asking?"

He couldn't ask yet, and he couldn't say *I shall next week* because that was as good as asking. But he couldn't bring himself to say no, either. He whirled away and began setting up his table to juice pineapple.

"You have so many responsibilities already," she said softly. "I didn't want to be one."

Robert leaned his fists on the counter, shutting his eyes. He could feel her drawing closer, feel the distance between them lessening until she put her arms around him and leaned her cheek on his back.

"I should have been more honest," she said. "But…it hurts. It hurts that now you think you've ruined me. That before I merited—I don't know, some kind of respect or care, or had some value that now I…don't, I suppose, in your eyes. There are two kinds of women, aren't there? Good women, who have to be protected from everything, and bad women, who can do as they like. And both of them get murdered."

Her chin dug into his back. "You'll probably say I've softened my brain with bad reading, but it's true. Girls are murdered for bedding men, and for refusing to."

"I'm not going to murder you!"

"That isn't the point. A woman can't win either way. And I wanted to do as I liked. For once in my small boring life." She sighed, her breasts moving against him. "But I'm sorry I wasn't honest. You'd a right to do as you like, too, and if you didn't want to be entangled with me…"

"I did want it," he said. "But I don't have to do everything I want to."

"You don't do anything you want to."

He jerked away from her, voice rising. "I've only ever done

what I wanted to!"

Only after heaving a crate of pineapples onto his table with a *thunk* could he speak at a reasonable volume again. "All I ever wanted was this shop, and I've been completely selfish about it. You must see that. I left my mother behind. I risked my father's patrimony. The Makepeaces saved for Peter's apprenticeship all their lives, and I should have told them, 'Find someone more established, I can't promise to be in business five years,' but I took their money!"

Robert twisted the crown off a pineapple with a savage jerk of his wrist. "I've taken a fortune from the Dymonds. I knew Mrs. Dymond was desperate and didn't want me, and I'd have married her anyway."

He set the fruit on its side and picked up his knife—and then he set it down, because his hand was shaking. "Don't you see how selfish I've been with *you*? You know those children who come in here and cry and scream because they don't understand why they can't have every sweet they set eyes on? That's what I've been like about this damned shop."

"You're allowed to *want* things," she said pleadingly.

He couldn't look at her. He couldn't look at her green-gold eyes and her sweet face and her yellow hair because he wanted her more than he'd ever wanted anything in his life.

Suddenly he remembered her lying on her back, that farthing of sunshine on her shoulder and a pattern of leaves on her face. *Your worst fear is losing the shop, isn't it?*

But it had stopped being, he realized. He was more afraid of losing her.

You can do this, he told himself. *Pick up the knife. Cut the pineapple. Make the ices and get your money. Then you can ask her to stay.*

His hands wouldn't stop shaking.

"You're allowed to want things," she repeated, more strongly, and came behind him again. This time she slid a hand down to his cock. "May I?"

Desire sprang to life, like hunger at the smell of food. He wanted this, and he lacked the will to deny himself. "Yes," he said. "Please."

Unbuttoning his breeches, she fondled him until he was hard and eager in her hand. Robert struggled to breathe, in and out, as her other hand reached round to cup his bollocks.

I'm allowed to want this, he told himself, and tried to believe it.

Letting go his bollocks, Betsy pushed his breeches down. She ran her hand over his arse, squeezing. "You've got a lovely arse."

"Thank you," he said.

She giggled, sounding almost happy again. Her hand drifted inwards, pushing one buttock aside to…to look at him? She circled his arsehole with her thumb, still stroking his cock. "If I were a man, I could put my cock in your fundament."

He froze. "What?"

"Isn't that what men do together?" She pushed up his shirt and kissed his bare back. "They wouldn't do it if it didn't feel good, don't you think?"

"Well, I imagine it feels good for the man doing the buggering." But her fingertip trailed over his arsehole again, and he shivered, his muscles contracting.

"I know, but…some men must like it, don't you think? I like it when you're inside me."

In spite of himself, he thought about it. If she were a man behind him and he loved that man the way he loved her, and her cock was pressing at his hole…he'd want it. He'd want her inside.

"You can't really mean to put your fingers in there."

She wavered. Then she let go of him and leaned past, arm outstretched. He caught half her smile out of the corner of his eye, and she plucked the pestle from the mortar.

All right, so it wasn't the great wooden bowl and club he'd mash the pineapple in, but neither was it the teacup-sized one for spices. The marble pestle was six inches long and slightly tapered, maybe an inch across at the narrow end.

Robert tingled all over, as sudden and sharp as if he'd just remembered a cake left in the oven.

He turned his head to see where she'd gone, and saw her smearing soft butter on the pestle with her fingers. The narrow end, thank God.

Would he really let her do this?

It was immoral, and probably against the law. Yet it seemed harmless enough in the sunny kitchen, and his cock stood stiffer than ever. Who knew why, but he wanted this—maybe badly.

I'm allowed to want things. Betsy says so.

So he stayed where he was, hands on the edge of the counter, breeches about his ankles, and let her caress his arse with slippery fingers. Planting his legs, he stared at the wood grain in the counter. The pestle poked at him, and it took him a moment to realize he had to relax and let it in.

Oh, that was strange, to feel it slip in an inch, propping him open. Betsy moaned as if she'd just taken her first taste of a new sweet. She pushed up his shirt and laid a line of openmouthed kisses down his spine, and somehow he opened farther. Butter dripped obscenely down his thighs.

It wasn't comfortable, but it was—it was *something*. The cool, unyielding marble was impossible to ignore. He was pinned here in this place, in this moment, every sensation heightened the way a splash of lemon woke up your taste buds.

Betsy laid her cheek between his shoulder blades and reached for his cock again, setting up a rocking motion behind as she tugged before.

The strange rhythmic pressure in his arse suddenly flooded his body with pleasure. It was too much at once, he couldn't bear it long—Robert wrapped his fist around hers and thrust with fierce purpose. He made sounds he was sure were ridiculous, crushing her fingers around his cock.

"Betsy," he got out. "Betsy—"

When she licked her lips, the tip of her tongue brushed his back. "Robert." She said his Christian name a little shyly. Her skirts caressed his bare legs every time she jolted gently forward.

He spilled over their fingers with a shout, his arse spasming helplessly around marble.

Robert squeezed his eyes shut and covered his face in his hands.

Betsy slipped the pestle out with a squelching, buttery sound. Ugh. His body was too worn out for mortification to spread much ice through his veins, though. His back made a popping sound as he straightened. "I'd better…clean up," he muttered, and escaped upstairs.

As he washed himself, he noticed for the first time how bare and dull his room was. It had never been strongly colored by any emotion but worry.

All his joy and pleasure and love and friendship, all the messy glory of life, was saved for the kitchen and the shop. Oh, he took himself in hand plenty of nights, but that hardly made a room feel lived in.

What would it be like to bring life here too?

He'd told Betsy he wanted the Honey Moon to make people feel as if they were in a happy home. But how could it, without being a happy home itself? *His* happy home.

Maybe his two dreams were intertwined, and he could have both of them. "I'm allowed to want things," he whispered to the empty room.

When he came downstairs and picked up his knife, his hand didn't shake at all. He started cutting pineapple.

CHAPTER 7:
Monday

B etsy walked to the Honey Moon just before dawn on Monday. She kept a lookout for murderers, but not a very sharp one; the sky was a rich, dark blue and the air was crisp and cool.

Robert smiled at her as she hung her pelisse on the peg, his face mysterious and dear in the dim light from the ovens. He was already clarifying sugar in a copper pot. He leaned over to kiss her as she walked by, but made no move to turn the kiss into anything more.

Betsy wasn't surprised. She'd seen his list of everything they needed to accomplish today: the custards and compositions for ices and ice creams, to chill overnight before being congealed tomorrow; macaroons for the grand trifle; blancmange and pistachio cream for the temple; molded jellies dotted with cherries and plums; crusts they would fill with sugared strawberries and whipped cream at the assembly.

If they finished it all, maybe tonight there would be time for dalliance, but they both already knew they wouldn't finish it all. They might not even sleep tonight. Betsy had warned her mother not to look for her.

If I do well today, he'll see what a good wife I'd make.

Suddenly the familiar thought made her uncomfortable.

All this week she'd striven to be the perfect woman, just as she'd striven for the last year and a half to be the perfect shopgirl. When Robert asked her what she was afeared of, she'd known without hesitation: *not being good enough.*

But could love really be earned like wages?

The ovens hadn't yet heated the room. Betsy felt cold and small.

She didn't want to live for his praise and his approval. She wasn't a child trying to make her mother smile anymore. If she meant to do this job for the rest of her life, she'd better enjoy it.

And as the day wore on, she found to her surprise that she *did* enjoy it. She liked the precision of it, and the beauty. She liked the lovely shining picture clarified sugar made when you poured it out. She liked the clinks of spoons in bowls and the thuds of spoons in pots. She liked the copper molds. She was glad she'd polished them to a shine.

She hadn't even noticed she was happy here, she'd been so busy thinking, *Is he happy?*

Could she really bring herself to leave, if he didn't propose at the end of the week?

When the clock struck one, Betsy was dropping neat spoonfuls of batter onto trays while Robert tended the ovens. She popped a warm macaroon in her mouth, feeling almost smug at how well things were going.

Someone knocked on the back door.

The dismay on Robert's face matched her own, but he

went and opened it, pasting on a smile. "Mrs. Lovejoy! How do you do?"

"Very well, Mr. Moon, and you?"

"Well, ma'am. I can only talk a moment, there's macaroons in the oven."

"Of course, of course," she said with a nervous laugh. "I've only a teensy-weensy little change to the menu."

Betsy's heart sank.

"What sort of change, ma'am?"

"Well…" Her face brightened. "It's good news, really. Wonderful news. The new Lord Ilfracombe is coming to our assembly. Just think! A tragedy of course; his father and two older brothers died quite suddenly. Now we have vaccination against smallpox, these things ought not to happen anymore, don't you agree? They were in a sailing accident, I believe. His lordship was quite good friends with the Dymond boy in the army, so he's coming here on his way home from the Peninsula. I just spoke to Mr. Nicholas and he said his friend will certainly attend our assembly. Such a chance for one of our girls! I hear he is to have quite six thousand a year. But he absolutely does not eat pineapple, Mr. Nicholas says. His mouth swells dreadfully. So we'll have to get rid of the pineapple ices."

Betsy set down her spoon. They had spent hours and quite a few guineas on the pineapple ices. The composition was cooling in the next room in a great copper bowl. Robert had to tell her no.

"I don't, um…" Robert looked pale and panicked. Silence stretched.

The last time Betsy had said something, she'd only made things worse. But she was the shopgirl, and it was her job to deal with customers. "That's wonderful! And it was you who invited him?"

Mrs. Lovejoy preened a little. "When Mr. Nicholas told me he was coming, I knew I couldn't let such a chance slip through my fingers. I owed it to the town."

"That was right kind of you," Betsy said. "I can't imagine how excited all the gentlemens' daughters will be."

Mrs. Lovejoy's eyes narrowed. "Don't *you* go talking to him, mind. I won't have him bothered."

"Mrs. Lovejoy," Robert said, exasperated.

And there it went, the little store of goodwill she'd built up in those few seconds to make their explanations go down smoother. Betsy wondered for the millionth time what she had done to make Mrs. Lovejoy dislike her.

"I wouldn't dream of it, ma'am," she said humbly. "I've got a fellow already."

Robert, bless him, didn't do anything too obvious with his face.

"Hmph," Mrs. Lovejoy said, sounding a little mollified. "Well, I hope you're behaving yourself, dear. This is a respectable establishment, and you've a responsibility to do nothing to tarnish it."

Betsy almost laughed. If she only knew! "I know, ma'am."

"Mrs. Lovejoy," Robert began firmly, ears red, "I'm going to have to ask you—"

"Mr. Moon," Betsy pleaded.

"Don't interrupt your betters, dear," Mrs. Lovejoy said.

Somehow, that knocked the breath out of her. *He is not my better*, she wanted to say. *He isn't.* But she couldn't speak.

"Betsy, if you would allow me to speak to Mrs. Lovejoy alone," Robert said.

Betsy hoped he wouldn't agree not to serve pineapple. She'd ought to hope he wouldn't read their customer a jobation, but at the moment, she hadn't the heart. "Yes, Mr. Moon," she said in a stifled voice. "I'll just go clean up some things in the front."

She went through the door to the front of the shop, and then leaned her ear against it.

"Thank you," Mrs. Lovejoy said. "I'm sorry, but something about that girl sets my back up."

"I've noticed, ma'am. But Betsy's done nothing to deserve it, and I'm hardly her better."

"You picked the right profession, that's all I can say." Mrs. Lovejoy's voice was already softening. "You're too sweet. Not her better! Your father was a shopkeeper, and hers was a workman."

Betsy's face burned, but the funny side of it occurred to her suddenly. How angry, how shocked Mrs. Lovejoy would be if she knew that yesterday Betsy had buggered Robert on the counter she was now leaning against!

"That's as may be, ma'am. But I've got to ask you to be kinder to her. I'd like her to stay a good long while."

Betsy's heart swelled. He did love her. She knew he did.

"You aren't sweet on her, are you? You heard her say she's got a fellow. No doubt some rough, loutish—oh, dear, if you could see your face! Very well, I won't be cattish."

"Thank you, ma'am," Robert said with a surprising lack of stammering. "Now about the pineapple."

"Please don't be difficult about this. It would mean ever so much to me."

"Did Mr. Nicholas ask you to take pineapple off the menu?"

"Oh, no, of course not! He's a young man, isn't he? Young

men have no consideration for each other. 'He's used to it,' he said. 'He'll be fine so long as he doesn't eat any.' But I do so want his lordship to be comfortable."

"Here's the way of it, ma'am. We've already bought the pineapples from Lord Wheatcroft, and juiced them, and done everything for the ices but congeal them. We haven't time to make a substitution before tomorrow night. It's only the one flavor of ice. There'll be many other things the baron can eat."

"I'm sure I don't want to be any trouble," Mrs. Lovejoy said, "but I can't have pineapple at the assembly."

"I've borrowed fifty pineapple molds from Lenfield. The pineapple ices will even *look* like pineapples, so there'll be no chance of mistake. We'll keep only five out on the sideboards at a time, with the rest hidden in the ice chests below."

"I'd really prefer another flavor."

"I know, ma'am, and I'm that sorry, but there just isn't time to make the change."

There was a long silence. "You haven't been very accommodating on this order," Mrs. Lovejoy said. "And it's a large one."

Betsy pressed her fist to her mouth to keep the bitterness in, the endless accommodations they'd made parading before her eyes. They'd closed the shop for a *week* to take this order.

"I've tried my best, ma'am." Robert sounded tired. "I truly have. I'm sorry I haven't satisfied you."

"You can serve the pineapple ice at the market this week," Mrs. Lovejoy said. "But it won't be at my assembly. I'm going to have to insist on this. Mr. Whittle at the Lost Bell told me he could provide the food for less money, you know. I told him no, because it wouldn't be the same—he always overcooks his roasts, have you noticed? But he *could*."

How *dare* she? Strangling was too good for that woman! If Mrs. Lovejoy walked out…there would be no more cream. No more butter. The sugar dealer had been rumbling about his bill, and the iceman.

"Very well, ma'am," Robert said flatly. "No pineapple. But it puts me out several guineas. I hope you'll remember that, and pay my bill promptly."

"If I'm happy tomorrow, I'll pay you on the spot."

You're never happy, Betsy thought.

"What is that smell?"

Robert cursed, and there was a clatter of footsteps across the kitchen.

"Language, Mr. Moon!"

"Beg pardon, ma'am."

There'd been only one tray in the oven. They'd have enough macaroons. But Robert so hated to burn things.

His face must have been dreadful, because Mrs. Lovejoy said, "Oh dear, the poor little things! I'd best go before I spoil anything else. No pineapple, mind," and a moment later the door shut behind her.

Robert didn't even look up from the burned biscuits when Betsy came into the room. Mouth a tight line, he strode jerkily to the door to toss them on the rubbish heap.

"I'm sorry," Betsy said, a lump in her throat. "All that lovely pineapple syrup."

He slammed the tray down hard on the counter. "The Lost Bell! Damn her and damn Lord Ilfracombe. The whole of yesterday afternoon. *And* the trip to Wheatcroft. Every hostess in England wants pineapple ices at their parties! They'd have been a roaring success. I ought to have told her no. I ought to have looked her in the eye and said no. Mr. Whittle can't make food for two hundred and twenty-five afore tomorrow."

"If he don't mind shutting his doors for a day, he can," Betsy said. "He cooks for two hundred and twenty-five every day in the week. You were splendid. I thought she'd give in, certain-sure."

He still didn't look at her. "I'll fetch out the sweet preserved lemons. We'll have to make fifty ices out of them." At the door the cold room, he paused. "She was wrong. If anything, you're *my* better."

The compliment didn't please her; he only said it because he esteemed himself low. But there was no use talking about it. Nothing would comfort him now but getting something done.

Picking up her spoon, Betsy began scooping out a fresh tray of macaroons.

CHAPTER 8:

Tuesday

"This'll be naught but salt water in a minute," Jemima said.

Betsy hurried over to show her how to let the water run out the bottom of the sabotiere so she could fill it up with ice again. It was the day of the assembly, and the kitchen was crammed with people churning syrup and custard into ices. Robert was hurrying about offering instructions and putting the finishing touches on his Greek temple.

They'd been naked here, and now it was a public place again.

He stirred a pot of hot sugar. The back of his neck and the curve of his ear made a wave of love wash over her.

It will all come right, she told herself. After this week, they'd be done with Mrs. Lovejoy. They'd have their money in hand, they'd sell the pineapple ices at the market, and she'd tell him she wanted to get married. She didn't need to wait, any more than she'd needed to wait for him to kiss her.

Robert picked up the heavy pot in his strong arms and began to slowly pour the hot sugar, tinted with indigo, into the ornamental pool.

There was an unpleasantly familiar rap on the door. Robert winced, but the thin, even stream of sugar didn't falter.

Betsy looked at the door. Oh, why hadn't she latched it? She *always* latched it! But there were so many people in the shop this morning. She must have forgotten after Nan went for a cup of coffee.

If Betsy latched it now, Mrs. Lovejoy would hear. She would never forgive the slight.

"I can't talk to her until this is done and I've got the fish in," Robert said tightly. "I can't stop neither, or it won't look right. It won't be but a moment. Take her round the front and tell her I'll be right there."

What could go wrong with that? Straightening her shoulders, Betsy slipped out the door and shut it behind her, blinking in the bright sun. Mrs. Lovejoy looked hot and tired even under her cheerful fringed parasol.

"Good day, Mrs. Lovejoy."

"Good day, child. Where's your master?"

"He's working hot sugar and can't stop just now, ma'am, but he'll be round to talk to you in a moment. Let me show you into the front of the shop where it's cooler."

"Oh, he needn't stop, I've only a very small question for him. Just you open that door and I'll be in and out before you can say Jack Robinson."

"I can't, ma'am, he asked me most particularly to show you into the shop. He's working hot sugar, ma'am. It isn't safe for you." Betsy was despairingly aware that the cheer in her voice rang a bit hollow.

Mrs. Lovejoy frowned. "There's no need to talk to me as if I were an infant, girl. I'm twice your age and I've been in a kitchen before. I won't do anything foolish."

Betsy tried to smile. "I'm sure you wouldn't, ma'am, but he's my master and those were his orders. Please come this way. It won't be but a moment."

Flattening herself against the wall, she tried to begin lead-ing the way round to the front of the building. But Mrs. Lovejoy was standing rather close, and as Betsy edged along the wall, her head bumped the matron's parasol. They both reached up to steady it, Betsy's hand knocked into Mrs. Lovejoy's, and the parasol went flying.

Mrs. Lovejoy drew back, clutching her wrist with a red face. "How dare you lay hands on me?"

Betsy's heart sank. She rushed to pick up the parasol. There were great dusty streaks. She didn't dare try to brush them off, for fear of being blamed for stains.

More than she already would be, anyway. "I'm that sorry, ma'am, I didn't mean to."

Mrs. Lovejoy didn't take the parasol. She was bending her wrist back and forth as if it might be injured, and rubbing her shoulder where the handle had bounced off it. "You may have your master fooled with that cringing air, girl, but I see through you!"

Hot hate spurted up in Betsy's heart. Mrs. Lovejoy bullied her, and then scolded her for taking it! But she *would* look cringing to anyone watching: a fluffy little dog at Mrs. Lovejoy's feet, fetching her parasol and hoping not to get kicked.

She dropped her eyes to hide her anger, but maybe she wasn't fast enough. "You know, I always thought you had some-thing against *me*," Mrs. Lovejoy said, light dawning in her face, "but I begin to think you're only an impertinent little hypocrite. And it is my duty to inform Mr. Moon of your true nature."

Robert came round the corner in time to hear this last bit. "I'm that sorry, ma'am, I looked for you in the front of the shop."

Betsy drew back against the wall and hoped with all her soul that Mrs. Lovejoy would just ask what she'd come to ask.

Mrs. Lovejoy drew herself up. "Your girl actually had the nerve to put her hands on me," she said. "She has damaged my property, and she is pert and two-faced. You may be too kind to see it, but you do her no favors by allowing her to continue in her shiftless ways. I demand, absolutely demand, that you dismiss her at once!"

Robert blinked, his brows drawing together. "Mrs. Lovejoy—"

The fussy curls at Mrs. Lovejoy's temples trembled. "I'm sorry, sir, but it is sack her or I cancel my order. I hate to do it, for I don't know what I shall do about the assembly, but I cannot in conscience allow myself to be treated in such a manner."

She snatched her parasol from Betsy at last; it shook in her hand, the fringe jumping. "Oh, Mr. Lovejoy will be furious with me, and what will everyone eat? But one must have self-respect, Mr. Moon."

Betsy looked at the horror written across Robert's face. If Mrs. Lovejoy cancelled the order now…they could never sell that much food in time. It would spoil, or the texture would go. Even an ice could only last so long. All those gallons of cream bought on credit, for nothing.

Your worst fear is losing the shop, isn't it?

I reckon so.

His throat worked, and his ears began to burn. Poor kind Robert. She wouldn't make him find the words.

Betsy untied the strings of her apron and pulled it off. "Good-bye, then."

"Wait," he said quietly.

She couldn't look at him. "It's all right. I don't mind."

He shook his head. "One must have self-respect, mustn't one, Mrs. Lovejoy?" She had never heard him sound like that: resolute as a Christian martyr. He looked their customer straight in the face. "I've done everything you asked. But I won't do this. I'd rather go bankrupt."

Mrs. Lovejoy looked as horrified as Betsy felt, with none of the helpless, guilty relief. "What will I tell Mr. Lovejoy?"

"That's up to you," Robert said. "Unless you'll change your mind. Everything's almost ready. It's going to be beautiful. Come in and see the temple."

Mrs. Lovejoy hesitated. Betsy sent up a quick prayer...but the woman wrung her hands and hurried off.

Leaving Betsy and Robert standing there, staring at each other.

"You shouldn't have done it," Betsy said, feeling almost shy. "I was ready to go."

He shook his head. "The shop's no use without you."

Joy poured over her. "The shop will be fine." She reached for his hand. "We'll sell as much of this as we can, and we'll make enough to pay Mrs. Diplock. We can preserve the berries—"

He shook his head again, and this time she saw the hopelessness in the motion. "Didn't you hear me? I'm going bankrupt."

"What?"

"I'm going bankrupt. The shop's over."

Her heart was ice trying to beat. Bankrupt? He was giving up on the shop? What chance did *she* have, if he'd given up on that?

"I won't run up any more debts I can't pay. If they don't send me to prison, I'll go work in someone else's kitchen.

Lenfield House, maybe. I can't ask you to wait, but in a few years…" He ducked, turning his head away. "Maybe I can save up enough to ask you to marry me."

"Why wait? If you want to marry me, why not now?"

"I can't ask you that."

"You can't ask me much, seems like."

"Betsy…"

She gathered up her courage. "I want to be your wife," she said. "Your helpmeet. I'm not going to change my mind. I don't mind not having money."

"I can't bring a wife to Lenfield with me."

"Don't go bankrupt," she couldn't help saying. They could come round. She knew they could. "We can—"

He turned his head away, showing her only that monklike profile. "Don't."

"Then I'll live in Lively St. Lemeston while you go to Lenfield. I don't mind waiting, if we're married."

"I can't."

Her eyes stung. "I've waited so long," she said around the lump in her throat. "I thought you'd come round eventually. But I was stupid. I can't earn your love. I can't demand you repay mine, like a debt. Either you love me or you don't. Either you want to marry me or you don't. But I won't wait anymore."

She took his hand, despite his sound of protest. "I'm good enough to be happy, and so are you, Robert. Let's—let's be happy."

"I do love you." He gripped her fingers. "I do want to marry you. Of course I do. But I can't ask you—do you realize, if we were married, you'd be liable for my debts?"

Betsy tried to be stoic. After all, she'd been ready for it

all week, hadn't she? Jemima would be disgusted if she broke down now.

Tears streamed down her face anyway. "You care so much whether I like your cake, and now I tell you I love you and it doesn't matter to you at all! I thought of the Honey Moon as ours, but of course I was just fooling myself. One must have self-respect? I'm sick when I think how little self-respect I've had."

She ripped her hand out of his, crumpling her apron into a ball. "*Your* shop, *your* happy home, *your* self-respect, *your* nerves that need soothing. What about my nerves? What about my heart that's breaking? I might as well have poured my love into a stone as into you and this blasted shop. You should have sacked me."

Betsy threw the apron at him. "Send my wages when you have them. If you ever have them."

Hand on the wall for balance, she went blindly toward the street, leaving her mother and sister and best friend inside still working. They were helping for free, because even though none of them had said anything, they all thought of it as an investment in the rest of Betsy's life.

Let Robert explain to them. She went home and crawled into her and Nan's bed and cried and cried.

Robert sat in his empty kitchen, tears leaking down his face. He might as well put out the fires entirely. He shrank from it, though. An oven without hot charcoal at the bottom of it was dead.

Everything was over. The shop and Betsy, and all because

he didn't have the patience God gave a grasshopper. He'd rushed everything. He should have waited to sell his father's bakery and saved up something. He should have taken on less debt, started on a quieter street, sold fewer kinds of candy, told Mrs. Lovejoy he wouldn't shut the shop for her order, told Betsy not to kiss him.

He definitely shouldn't run after her now and beg her to marry him.

He knew all of that was true. And yet when he thought, *I should have told Betsy not to kiss me*, every last drop of blood in him dug in its heels. He just…couldn't really believe that.

He'd made a great many mistakes. But maybe…maybe he'd just made the worst of them.

He washed his face, banked the fires, and ran out the door.

Robert knew which house she lived in, but not which room. He didn't want to embarrass her. He hesitated for half a minute, and then gave it up as a bad job.

"Miss Piper!" he bellowed. "Miss Piper!"

It was July; all the sashes were open. He knew she must have heard him. Curious faces poked out of windows all up and down the street.

Face burning, he shouted again, "Miss Piper, I need to talk to you!"

A minute or two passed in silence. He was gathering breath to shout again when someone came round the back of the house.

It was Jemima Midwinter, scowling. He tried to decide if this was better or worse than no one coming at all. Better, he decided. "Let me see her," he said, trying to sound commanding.

It was no good. She crossed her arms. "Why should I?"

"It's not your affair." Oh, why had he said that? Her glower heated by a few hundred degrees. He shrank back.

"I think people hurting my bosom friend *is* my affair, and I think you'd better get out of here before I'm on trial for bashing your head in."

He'd always suspected that Miss Midwinter's fascination with murder was bloodthirstier than Betsy's. He swallowed. "I want to marry her."

"Yes, she mentioned that. Only you can't ask her to wait. Sounds like a lot of excuses to me."

"I'm not asking her to wait." He took a deep breath. "I'm asking her if we can post the banns this Sunday." Saying it felt like diving into cold water on a hot day, the way you came up to the surface shocked and laughing.

She blinked. "Really?"

He nodded. "And…er…of course you'd be welcome in our home whenever you liked?"

Miss Midwinter raised her eyebrows. "How generous of you." She chewed her lip. "You promise? About the banns?"

"I'll take my oath, if you've got a Bible about you."

She shrugged, turning and walking back the way she'd come. He followed her into the back garden, through a cramped kitchen, and up a flight of stairs to the Pipers' room. It was homey, with pictures tacked to the wall, and that was all he had time to notice because Betsy sat on one of the beds, eyes red with tears. Her mother and sister watched him silently from either side of her.

"What do *you* want?" Betsy asked, voice thick.

"I changed my mind."

She went white as powdered sugar. "What?" she whispered.

"I changed my mind. Can we...can we talk in private?"

"You don't have to," Miss Midwinter told her. "I could push him down the stairs instead."

Nan, sitting beside Betsy, gave her a gentle nudge in his direction and whispered something in her ear.

"You'd better not make my daughter cry again, young man," Mrs. Piper said.

Betsy sniffled behind her handkerchief. "Why don't you talk to me here," she said. "Jemima might need witnesses. You know, that it was an accident."

He looked at her blotchy, wary face. He'd never wanted *anything* so much. "I changed my mind," he said again. "I've been as bad as Mrs. Lovejoy, haven't I? Expecting to get the things I want *now*, and just the way I like them, and if I don't, I'll pack up my things and go."

He got to his knees, so her face would be closer. "While I'm at it, I'm that sorry about Mrs. Dymond. It was a mistake to think of marrying her. It was counter to everything I want to do with the shop, and I'd have been unhappy. But that isn't the worst of it, is it? It was cruel to you. I didn't understand how much it hurt you, but I did—I did know you liked me, and I'm sorry."

Jemima snorted.

"No," Betsy told her. "It feels nice to hear him admit it."

"I shouldn't have taken Mrs. Lovejoy's order, and I knew it when I took it, but I took it anyway, because I wanted—" He remembered suddenly. "Because I wanted to marry you quicker."

Her mouth made a small round O, and her eyes flew to his face—but only for a moment, a flash of green and honey.

"I got myself into this pickle," he said, "and here I am asking you to go snacks with me. But…"

It wasn't easy to go on, not knowing how she'd take his words. But at the same time, he couldn't understand how, but it *was* easy. Maybe because he knew what he felt, and nothing could change it.

"I've never been so happy as I was with you this week, and it made me afeared. Of losing it, aye, but not deserving it too, I reckon. Not sufficing. Not paying it back." He didn't think of all the people he wasn't going to pay back. Shops went bankrupt sometimes. That was life.

He thought about Betsy, and what she wanted, because they were both allowed to want things. "Happiness hadn't ought to frighten a man. He should be strong enough for it. Strong enough for sorrow too. I love you, and to hell with it. You're a grown woman, aren't you? You know what you're risking, and you can say yes or no as you like, but I'm asking you. Will you marry me? If you say yes we'll post the banns on Sunday and be married inside a month."

Nan make a small squealing nose, and Jemima sighed in resignation. But Betsy met his gaze, finally, and he sagged with relief at the look in her eyes. "You mean it, don't you?" she said. "Please mean it. Oh drat, I've used up my handkerchief."

He gave her his. "I mean it."

She threw herself into his arms. Her lips tasted like salt, but it was a wonderful kiss. A kiss that didn't have to lead to anything naughtier, that was just a kiss, just a way of saying how he felt about her.

She kissed him back, wordlessly telling him she felt the same. He expanded into light and air until he thought he might split open, like a meringue put in an oven too hot for it. But he didn't. He was strong enough for this. She trembled, and he rubbed her back until she stopped.

When he could stop kissing her, her mother and sister cried and embraced her. Jemima Midwinter embraced her too, and regarded him over Betsy's shoulder with a flat, menacing *Don't make me regret this* look.

Robert beamed at her.

"Don't—don't sell the shop," Betsy said suddenly. "Please. I think we can save it."

He blinked, afraid again. It was one thing to be gloriously happy, but to be gloriously happy twice over... "Do you think so?"

"She as good as runs that shop," Jemima said. "I'd trust her opinion over yours."

"*Jemima.* I love the Honey Moon," she told him. "I hate the thought of it being gone."

He took a deep breath. "All right," he told her. "If that's what you want."

"We'll sell everything at the market tomorrow. It will be an awful hot day."

"Pfft," Mrs. Piper said. "Go tonight and set up a cart outside the Assembly Rooms. Everyone will be hungry enough, you could charge double."

His eyes met Betsy's. The awed expression on her face probably matched his own.

"Could we really?" she said, almost wistfully. "Mrs. Lovejoy will be furious."

He shrugged. "Then she shouldn't have canceled her order." He looked around the room. "Would you all mind awfully coming back to the shop for a few hours?"

"Ices," Betsy called out. "Cold ices for a shilling! Pineapple, lemon, peach, coffee ices! Trifle! Blancmange! Jellies! Burnt cream!"

Robert settled the blancmange dome atop the temple, grinning when it balanced. It looked magnificent, and a small crowd had already gathered to watch.

Betsy thought privately that Robert looked magnificent too.

It was a hot night, especially for gentlemen in evening dress. Young Lord Wheatcroft, handsome in his black tails, stopped to buy an ice. His sister and her husband hung back, too staunchly Tory to have ever come in the shop.

"Made with our pineapples!" the baron told them proudly, and grinned at his sister. "You're red as a lobster, Lydia. Take care you don't swoon."

Mrs. Cahill did look hot even in frothy yellow muslin, her careful copper curls wilting at the back of her neck.

Betsy opened the ice chest halfway, sending cool air wafting in the lady's direction. Mrs. Cahill glanced indecisively at her husband, who tossed a shilling in the air and caught it before dropping it in Betsy's hand.

"A coffee ice, if you please," he said. "Thank you. Will you share it with me, Mrs. Cahill? That's only half a wickedness."

Mrs. Cahill's mouth curved up, and she whispered something in his ear that made them both laugh.

"You can borrow a spoon if you eat it here, sir," Betsy said.

Soon their little table was surrounded by gentlefolk in their Sunday best, eating ices with borrowed spoons and laughing and talking and not going inside at all. The Dymonds stopped to say good evening, and then stayed to wish Betsy and Robert joy, and the next thing Betsy knew, their friend the new Lord Ilfracombe had bought the entire sugar temple and spent most of an hour happily divvying up the choicest bits among himself, his friends, and attractive young ladies passing by.

It all felt rather like a fair, and no one showed any inclination to leave the cheerful open-air bustle for the stifling assembly rooms.

"That's three I owe you," Robert told the Dymonds ruefully.

Mr. Dymond looked surprised. "You know that was all my mother's money, don't you?"

Robert blinked.

"We'd rather you had it than her," Mrs. Dymond assured him, and for the first time, Betsy liked her. "Just vote Orange-and-Purple next election."

At last Mrs. Lovejoy appeared on the porch to find out what was keeping everyone. Seeing their cart, she flushed a hectic red, mouth trembling. Her eyes glistened. For a moment Betsy was afraid she'd come down and shout at them, and then she thought—*and what if she does?*

"We're getting married, ma'am!" she called cheerfully. Robert laughed and waved.

Mrs. Lovejoy jerked back as if she'd been slapped.

"Two raspberry ices, if you please," Jack Sparks said, pushing his wife up in her wheelchair, and by the time Betsy looked back up at the porch, Mrs. Lovejoy was disappearing inside, posture rigid.

"Thank you," Caroline Sparks said, eyes gleaming as she took a bite. "Firstly for this ambrosia, and secondly because this is much more fun than watching people dance." She passed Robert her memorandum book and a pencil. "Can you write down a copy of the menu for the paper?"

In a few hours, all that was left were a few drifts of cream, some overturned sugar pillars, and an empty crystal trifle bowl.

"Maybe I should go back to the shop and see if I can fetch anything out of the cupboard," Robert said. But the sun was setting, and after all that sugar the townsfolk were finally ready to dance; they drifted into the Assembly Rooms in twos and threes. Lord Ilfracombe wrapped the rock candy boulders in his handkerchief, kissed Betsy on the cheek, and went inside.

Robert and Betsy beamed tiredly at each other. "How much did we make?" he asked.

"Thirty pounds, five shillings, and sixpence," she said. "We ought to have charged *triple* for everything."

He shrugged. "It's more than enough to pay the milk-woman. What do you say we go home and wash all these spoons?"

But somehow they ended up splashing each other at the pump and then helping each other out of their wet things, and the spoons had to wait until morning.

EPILOGUE:
Wednesday

B etsy couldn't stop smiling as she opened the shop for the first time in a week. *This is mine now*, she thought, fussing over the small display of fresh-baked cakes and buffing the counter till it shone.

Mine, mine, mine, she hummed as she dusted each jar of candy in the window.

Mornings were slow, even on market day when folks came from out of town. She had plenty of time to get everything in order, maybe even take the jars down and really wash the window—

The doorbell jangled. In came a young matron with a nursemaid and a young boy of three or four. "Do you have any more of those lemon ices you were selling at the assembly last night?" she asked. "Peregrine was heartbroken to have missed them."

The boy smiled hopefully at Betsy.

Betsy smiled back. "No more lemon ices today," she told him. "But I promise we'll have more tomorrow. Do you think you might like a lemon cheesecake in the meantime?"

She polished the sixpence on her apron before she dropped it in the till. *Mine.*

The doorbell rang again. "I could barely sleep for thinking of that trifle," the new customer said. "Have you got any more?"

"Not with strawberries, but what would you say to peaches and Madeira?"

At eleven, Mr. Foley, the bookshop owner, stopped by for his wife's weekly seedcake. He looked around suspiciously. "When did it get so damned crowded in here?"

Robert carried a freshly glazed lavender cake through the door just in time to hear that. He smiled so wide Betsy thought her heart would burst.

"We'll just have to get used to it, Mr. Foley," he said. "Betsy's agreed to marry me, did she tell you?"

Author's Note

T hank you for reading *A Taste of Honey*! I hope you enjoyed Betsy and Robert's story.

Would you like to know when my next book is available? Sign up for my newsletter at roselerner.com, follow me on twitter at @RoseLerner, or find me on Facebook at https://www.facebook.com/roselernerromance.

Reviews help other readers find books. I appreciate all reviews, positive and negative.

This is book 4 in my series about the little market town of Lively St. Lemeston. Mr. Moon was first introduced in Book 1, *Sweet Disorder*, about Phoebe and Nick Dymond. Book 2, *True Pretenses*, is a marriage of convenience story about Ash and Lydia Cahill, who shared a coffee ice. Book 3, *Listen to the Moon*, is about Phoebe's irrepressible maid-of-all-work and Nick's very proper valet, who marry to get a plum job.

Visit my website for free short reads (including a ministory where Robert and Betsy compete on a reality baking show), plus *A Taste of Honey* DVD extras like Pinterest boards, recipes, and historical research. There's information about Regency ice cream, Sussex slang, shop window displays, box pews, and much more.

Turn the page to learn more about my other Regency romances.

MORE BOOKS BY
Rose Lerner

LIVELY ST. LEMESTON SERIES

Sweet Disorder
True Pretenses
Listen to the Moon

To find out when new Lively St. Lemeston books release,
sign up for my newsletter at roselerner.com!

NOT IN ANY SERIES

In for a Penny
A Lily Among Thorns
All or Nothing (a novella)

TURN THE PAGE for an excerpt from *Sweet Disorder*,
in which a wounded officer tries to find a husband for a
prickly widow to help win a local election.

Sweet Disorder

Campaigning has never been sweeter...

Prickly newspaperman's widow Phoebe Sparks has vowed never to marry again. Unfortunately, the election in Lively St. Lemeston is hotly contested, and the little town's charter gives Phoebe the right to make her husband a voter—if she had one.

The Honorable Nicholas Dymond has vowed never to get involved in his family's aristocratic politicking. But now his army career is over for good, his leg and his self-confidence both shattered in the war against Napoleon. Helping his little brother win an election could be just what the doctor ordered.

So Nick decamps to the country, under strict orders to marry Phoebe off to *somebody* before the polls open. He's intrigued by the lovely widow from the moment she shuts the door in his face.

Phoebe is determined not to be persuaded by the handsome earl's son, no matter how charming he is. But when disaster strikes her young sister, she is forced to consider selling her vote—and her hand—to the highest bidder.

As election intrigue thickens, bringing them face to face with their own deepest desires, Phoebe and Nick must decide which vows are worth keeping, and which must be broken...

Contains elections, confections, and a number of erections.

Chapter 1

Phoebe sat at the foot of her bed, her elbows propped on the deal table she'd placed under the window. She was supposed to be writing her next Improving Tale for Young People. But the shingled wall and gabled roof of Mrs. Humphrey's boarding house across the way were so much more absorbing than the tragic tale of poor Ann, who had been got with child by a faithless young laird and was now starving in a ditch.

If Phoebe strained, she could even see a sliver of street two stories below.

The problem was that she couldn't quite decide what would happen to Ann next. Tradition dictated that either the girl die there, or that her patient suffering inspire the young laird to reform and carry her off to a church, but…that was so *boring*. Every Improving Tale-teller in England had already written it. It had been old when Richardson did it seventy years ago.

But she couldn't afford to waste this precious time in daydreams. It was washing day, and Sukey, the maid she and her landlady shared with Mrs. Humphrey, would soon be back from her shopping to help. Then tomorrow Phoebe had to piece her quilt for the Society for Bettering the Condition of the Poor's auction in December, and what with one thing and another, she wouldn't have any more time to write until Tuesday. She had promised this story to the editor of the *Girl's Companion* in time for typesetting three weeks from now.

There were footsteps on the stairs and a knock at her door. *I do* not *feel relieved*, she thought firmly. Standing and crossing into her sitting room, she opened the door to discover—

"Mr. Gilchrist." She felt much less relieved.

The dapper Tory election agent stood at the top of the narrow spiral of stairs leading to her attic. A few drops of rain glistened in his sleek brown hair, on his broadcloth shoulders, and on the petals of the pink-and-white carnation—the colors of the local Tory party—in his buttonhole.

Drat. If it was raining, washing would have to be put off until she had Sukey again next Friday. And she'd have to keep a careful eye on the bucket under the leak in her roof to make sure it didn't overflow.

"Ah, you know of me," he said with an oily smile. "Pleased to make your acquaintance, Mrs. Sparks."

Oh, his smile is not *oily. Prejudice combined with the urge to narrate is a terrible thing.* She smiled back. "And I'm pleased to make yours. But I should warn you, I'm Orange-and-Purple, and so are my voting friends." There was a general election on in England to choose a new Parliament. While many districts could go decades with the same old MPs, the Lively St. Lemeston seats always seemed to be hotly contested.

He tilted his head. "Your father and your husband were Whigs. But from what I hear, you're an independent woman. Decide for yourself." His expression turned rueful. He couldn't be more than twenty. "Besides, it's starting to rain and I'd rather not go outside again just yet."

She sighed. He was good at this. "May I offer you some tea?"

"I'd love some."

Maybe his smile was oily after all. Phoebe went to take the kettle from the fire, but she didn't bring out the cheese rolls from the cupboard. They cost a penny each, and she wanted them for herself.

Mr. Gilchrist waited patiently while she topped off the teapot with hot water. She didn't add any tea. A second steeping was good enough for him.

"I know you're a busy and practical woman, so I'll come straight to the point," he said as she poured. "Thank you, I take it black." A politic choice, visiting a poor widow. "Under the Lively St. Lemeston charter, every freeman of the town has the right to vote for up to two candidates in an election."

"I know that, Mr. Gilchrist." Men always wanted to explain things, didn't they?

"Also under the Lively St. Lemeston charter," he continued, clearly having no intention of modifying his planned oration, "the eldest daughter of a freeman who died without sons can make her husband a freeman."

Phoebe tapped her foot on the floor. "My husband is dead," she pointed out, since apparently they were telling each other things they both already knew.

The young man took a sip of tea. He had an eye for a dramatic pause, anyway; she had to give him credit for that. "You could marry again."

She blinked. "What?"

"Mr. Dromgoole, our candidate, would be happy to assist in finding any prospective spouse a lucrative place in his chosen profession." His smile didn't falter. Definitely oily.

"You think I'm going to get *married* just to get you extra *votes*? The polls are in a month!" She set her still-empty teacup back on the table with a rattle.

"Allow me." He put a small lump of sugar into the cup, poured it half full of tea, and then filled it almost to the brim with milk.

"You found out how I like my tea?" she asked incredulously.

There was a hint of boyish smugness in his smile now. "I know how you like your men too. If you'll just meet my nominee—"

She stood. "How dare you? Get out of my house."

It wasn't her house, though. It was her two cramped attic rooms. His eyes drifted for a moment, letting that sink in, reminding her of how much more she could have if she married.

He might know how she liked her tea, but he didn't know a thing about her if he thought she'd be happier in a fine house that belonged to her husband. These two rooms were *hers*.

He rose. "I'll give you a few days to think it over. A message at the Drunk St. Leonard will always reach me."

She went to the door and jerked it open. "Even love wouldn't convince me to marry again. An election certainly won't." She'd always had a tendency to bend the truth in favor of a neat bit of dialogue. But *love wouldn't convince me to marry again unless I were sure it wouldn't become a bickering, resentful mess like the first time* just didn't sound the same.

Mr. Gilchrist shook his head mournfully and bounded down the stairs. He passed out of sight—and there was a squawk and the sound of bouncing fruit. "I'm dreadfully sorry," he said, not sounding very sorry.

Phoebe started down to help Sukey collect the groceries, turning the corner just in time to see the girl pocket something. "Pardon me, did you just bribe my maid?"

"It's not a bribe." Mr. Gilchrist tossed a couple of apples

back in the basket with unerring aim. "It's damages for the fruit."

She considered throwing an apple at him as he disappeared around the next bend, but even in October the fruit wasn't cheap enough to justify it. "The Orange-and-Purples would never stoop this low," she shouted after him instead.

"Don't count on it," Mr. Gilchrist called back.

"I hope he's right," Sukey said cheerily. "I could use another shilling."

Read the rest of Chapter 1 and buy the book at
roselerner.com/bookshelf/sweetdisorder.html

Made in the USA
Lexington, KY
12 April 2018